Donald G. Mitchell

Rural Studies

With hints for country places

Donald G. Mitchell

Rural Studies
With hints for country places

ISBN/EAN: 9783337228125

Printed in Europe, USA, Canada, Australia, Japan

Cover: Foto ©Andreas Hilbeck / pixelio.de

More available books at **www.hansebooks.com**

SPECIAL ANNOUNCEMENT.

MESSRS. C. SCRIBNER & Co. beg to announce that they
have in preparation a limited edition of

"MY FARM OF EDGEWOOD,"

TO BE ILLUSTRATED WITH

TEN PHOTOGRAPHIC VIEWS UPON THE FARM,

BY MR. ROCKWOOD, OF THIS CITY.

The edition will be limited in number, and will make a unique
and elegant volume in quarto form.

Early orders are solicited.

RURAL STUDIES

WITH

HINTS FOR COUNTRY PLACES.

BY THE AUTHOR OF

"MY FARM OF EDGEWOOD."

NEW YORK:

CHARLES SCRIBNER & CO.

1867.

JOHN F. TROW & CO.,
PRINTERS, STEREOTYPERS, AND ELECTROTYPERS,
50 Greene Street, New York.

PREFACE.

THIS little book does not treat exhauftively of any of the fubjects which are brought to view in its pages; it is more full of fuggeftion than inftruction. Its aim is to ftimulate thofe who live in the country, or who love the country, to a fuller and wider range of thinking about the means of making their homes enjoyable—rather than to lay down any definite rules by which this may be accomplifhed.

I have efpecially fought to excite the ambition of thofe holders of humbler eftates, who believe that nothing can be done in the way of adornment of country property, except under the eye of accomplifhed gardeners. I have endeavored fteadily to fhow—whatever may have been the divergence of topic—that the proper appliance of fmall means will produce effects whofe charms muft, in their way, ftand unrivalled, and that there is no neceffary gulf of diftinction in quality of beauty between the beft-ordered large eftate and the judicioufly ordered fuburban home of the mechanic.

When we learn to achieve and appreciate the beauties that are fimple, we fhall have no difficulty in achieving the beauties that are complex. The book is a tract for homelinefs; and I hope it may make country profelytes.

EDGEWOOD, May, 1867.

CONTENTS.

—

IV.—LAYING OUT OF GROUNDS.

V.—MR. URBAN AND A COUNTRY HOUSE.

AN OLD-STYLE FARM.

I.

AN OLD-STYLE FARM.

SOME twenty odd years ago—more or less—I chanced to be the owner of a wild, unkempt, slatternly farm, of three or four hundred acres in extent, amid the rocky fastnesses of eastern Connecticut. The township in which it lay was a scattered wilderness of a settlement, lying along the Hartford and New London turnpike. There was a toll-gate (I remember that), and I have a fancy that the toll-gatherer was a sallow-faced shoemaker with club-feet, who sometimes made his appearance with a waxed-end in his mouth, and a flat-headed hammer in his hand. He hardly wields the hammer any more ; and his last waxed-end must long ago have been drawn tight, and clipped away.

There was a wild common over which the November winds swept with a pestilent force, with nothing to break them, except a pair of twin churches. One

1

of these was Congregational—severely doric, with
square-headed windows, painted columns, and a cupola
for ornamentation. The other was Episcopal, with
sharp-headed windows, and three or four crazy-look-
ing turrets; but the paint upon this latter was nearly
worn away by the storm-gusts that beat unbroken
over the Common. I am compelled to say too that
the services were only occasional in this gothic taber-
nacle; and regret exceedingly to add that, after a
fitful and spasmodic life, the Episcopal society which
maintained nominal ownership of this turreted temple
made over its interest and debts to certain worldly
parties, and the sharp-headed windows now shed their
light upon " town meetings," and the late church is
abased to the uses of a town hall. It must be said,
that the rural residents of New England have no
large or growing appreciation of the beautiful Litany.
They like long sermons and a " talking out " in
prayer. You or I may feel differently; but the men
of the population in the retired districts, where books
and newspapers rarely come, want to hear on a Sunday what the parson will say—not only in his sermon,
but in his invocations.

The doric meeting-house, however, gloried in a
thick, white sheen of paint. The blinds were green
to a fault. No exterior mark of prosperity seemed
wanting but a flanking line of horse-sheds, the lack

of which upon that bare waste was a terrible source
of discomfort to the poor brutes who, after a drive
of three, four, or even five miles, stood shivering in
the December weather under the lee of the fences.
A good, kind parson, who presided over the parish
in the days of which I speak, was earnest in his appeals
for shelter to the poor brutes, (my little bay mare
often shivering among them,) but the charitable enthusiasm of the good minister counted for nothing;
and to this day, as I am credibly informed, the " con-
templated sheds " remain unbuilt.

There was a tavern, lying to the northward, along
the turnpike; and if I remember rightly, the tavern-
keeper was a deacon—a staid man, of course, who
kept an orderly house, and whose daughters, in flamboyant ribbons, were among the belles of the parish.
The father was, I believe, a most worthy man; but
his rusty brown wig showed badly beside the great
flock of golden curls that flanked him in his meeting-
house pew. His boys were absentees, and addicted
to horse-trading.

There was a cooper's shop upon the sprawling
street, in which a great clatter and bang were kept
up every work-day upon shad-barrels. There was
a carriage-repairing shop, whose restive proprietor
once brought suit against me for the non-payment
of a bill. (I am still perfectly satisfied, in my

own mind, that I paid twice for that "white-oak X.")

There was a green country store, where "domestics" were sold, and West India sugars, and hoes—"Ames' best cast-steel"—and, I greatly fear, occasional tipple. It was burned down long ago; ten years after, I saw the yawning, ragged cellar, and a giant growth of stramonium springing from the door-step.

There was also somewhere along this dreary street a manufactory of musical instruments—whether of harps or organs I cannot justly say; but I have been given to understand that the manufactory has since, under zealous and spirited management, grown into a great musical institute, where young misses in white (with blue sashes) woo the muses with a thundering success. But more distinctly than the manufactory —whatever it may have been—I remember a little brook, that stole away in the meadows thereabout under clumps of alder, under lines of willows, under plank bridgelets, and how, on many a May day my line drifted on into dark pools, until some swift strike gave warning of a venturesome, golden-spotted swimmer that presently tossed and flounced in my creel. I profess no great love for music—no knowledge of it even; but the whizzing of a reel which a pound trout will make at the end of thirty feet of taper line

is to me very charming—charming in those old days
when the woods and meadows were new, and charming now when the woods and the meadows are old.
Well, well, I began to tell the story of a farm, and
here I am idling along the borders of a brook!

The toll-gate, the churches, the tavern, the store
lay strewn along a high-road, three miles away from
the valley-farm, of which in those days I was busy
occupant. And yet so bare of trees was the interval,
that from many a nook under the coppices of the
pasture-land I could see the twin churches, the tavern,
and, with a glass, detect even a stray cow, or the lumbering coach which from time to time wended along
the high-road of the village.

The farm was suitably divided (as the old advertisements were wont to say) into tillage, meadow, and
pasture-lands. This distribution of parts implied that
the meadows would furnish enough hay in ordinary
seasons for the winter's keep of such and so many
animals, as the pastures carried in good condition
through the summer; and the arable land was supposed equal to the growth of such grain and vegetables as would suffice for man and beast throughout
the year. It was an old, lazy reckoning of capabilities, which implied little or no progress, and which
took no account of any systematic rotation. I never
see a farm advertised under the formula I have named

—suitably divided into tillage, mowing, and pasture-
land—but I feel sure that the advertiser is a respectable, old-fashioned gentleman, who keeps a long-tailed
black coat for Sundays and training-days, and who
has inherited his agricultural opinions from a very
dull and stiff-necked ancestry. Such announcements
—and they are to be seen not unfrequently in the
journals—impress me very much as the advertisement of a desirable dwelling might do—" suitably
divided into cooking, eating, and sleeping quarters."

There are, to be sure, rough pasture-lands strewn
with rocks, or full of startling inequalities of surface,
which must retain for an indefinite period their office
for simple grazing purposes ; but, with rare exceptions, there are not anywhere in the northeastern
States any considerable stretches of meadow capable
of growing the better English grasses, which are not
susceptible of improvement under occasional tillage.
Draining, indeed, may be first needed, and a scarify-
ing with the harrow, to root out the old mosses and
foul growth ; but after this, a clean lift of the plow
and judicious dressing will work wonders.

But, to return, (for I wish to make the picture of
an old-fashioned farm complete,) there were mossy
meadows lying along the borders of a great romping
millstream, which had been mown for forty years
without intermission ; here and there, where these

meadows lifted into gravelly mounds, patches of plowland had been taken up at intervals of five or eight
years, and by dint of heavy, laborious cartage of the
scant manures from the barnyard, over the intervening meadow "swales", had shown their periodic
growth of corn or potatoes, these followed by oats—
more or less rank as the season was wet or dry—and
again, on the following year by clover, which in its
turn was succeeded by red-top and timothy—upon
which the wild meadow-growth steadily encroached.

There was, of course, the "barn-lot," of which all
old farmers boasted, maintained in a certain degree
of foodful succulence and luxuriant fertility by reason
of the leakage and waste which it inevitably secured,
and whose richness was due rather to lack of care
than to skill. There were intervals too of meadow
upland, through which some little rivulet from the
pasture hill-side meandered on its way to the larger
brook of the lowland, and which were kept in verdant
wealth (no thanks to any human manager) by the
refreshing influences of the rivulets alone. Four or
five such straggling brooklets murmured down from
the pasture high-lands, and a Devonshire farmer
would have given to each one a wide and wealth-giv-
ing distribution over acres and acres of the slanting
meadows. But there was nothing of this. They
watered their little rod-wide margin of succulent

grasses, then dropped away into some marshy flat, where the flags and rushes grew rampantly, until these too gave place to alders, poison sumacs, soft maples and black-ash trees.

The fences were as motley as the militiamen's coats on a first Monday of May. From time to time some previous tenant or owner had devoted " fall leisure " to the erection of a wall—mostly in continuation of a great range of barrier which separated the hill-lands from the flat. In this erection each owner's views of economy (no other views being recognized) had taken wide divergence. Thus, one had given a circular sweep to his trail, for the sake of inclosing some tempting smooth spot upon the lowest slope of the hills ; another had made a flanking movement in the other direction, for the sake of excluding some unfortunate little group of innocent rocks. But the sinners and the well-doers, on the score of the walling, must have long before gone to their account, since the stones were all mossy, and the frequent gaps had been blocked up by lopping over some vigorous young hickory or chestnut which had started from the base of the wall.

But even this rustic device had not given full security, for with settlements and the " bulging " under frosts, this great line of barrier was no proof against the clambering propensities of the sheep ; and the whole line of fence had been topped with long poles, kept in their places by cross stakes firmly driven into the ground and sustaining the "riders" at the point of intersection. To complete the fence picture, I have to add to those half-lopped hickories in the gaps—to those bulging tumors of stone—to those gaunt over-riding poles—a great array of blackberry briers, of elders, of dog-willows, of dried stems of golden-rod, of raspberries, and of pretentious wild-cherries. Still further, I must mark down a great sprawling array of the scattered wall, in some half-dozen spots, where adventurous hunters had made a mining foray after some unfortunate woodchuck or rabbit.

So much for the average New England walling in retired districts twenty years ago. Is it much better now? As for the wooden fencing, there stretched across the meadow by the road a staggering line of "posts and rails"—one post veering southward the next veering northward—a wholly frightful line, which was like nothing so much as a file of tipsy soldiers making vain efforts to keep "eyes right." In the woodlands and upon the borders of the farm, were old, lichen-covered Virginia fences, sinking rail by rail into the earth; luxuriant young trees were shooting up in the angles, brambles were overgrowing them, and poisonous vines—the three-leaved Ampe-

1*

lopsis among them (which country people call mer-
cury, ivy, and I know not what names beside)—and
this entire range of exterior fence was gone over each
springtime—April being the usual month—and made
effective, by lopping upon it such lusty growth as
may have sprung up the season past. It is afflictive
to think what waste of natural resources is committed
in this way every year by the scrubby farmers of New
England !

The stock equipment of this farm of nearly four
hundred acres, consisted of twelve cows, some six
head of young stock, two yoke of oxen, a pair of
horses, and a hundred and fifty sheep. I blush even
now as I write down the tale of such poor equipment
for a farm which counted at least two hundred and
seventy acres of open land—the residue being wood,
or impenetrable swamp. And it is still more melancholy to reflect that the portion of the land which
aided most in the sustenance of this meagre stock,
was that which was most nearly in a state of nature.
I speak of those newly cleared pasture-lands from
which the wood had been removed within ten years.
In giving this description of a farm of twenty years
ago, I feel sure that I am describing the available
surface of a thousand farms in New England to-day.
We boast indeed of our thrift and enterprise, but
these do not work in the direction of land culture—

at least not in the way of that liberal and generous
culture which insures the largest product. I doubt
greatly if there be any people on the face of the
earth, equally intelligent, who farm so poorly as the
men of New England; and there are tens of thousands less intelligent who manage their lands infinitely
better. I do not quite understand why the American
character, which has shown such wonderful aptitude
for thrift in other directions, should have shown so
little in the direction of agriculture. I feel quite confident that seven out of ten of the most accomplished
and successful nurserymen, gardeners, and farmers in
the country, are of foreign birth, or of foreign parent-
age. Within the limits of my own experience, I find
it infinitely more difficult to secure a good American
farmer, than to secure a good Scotch or even an Irish
one. And I observe with not a little shame, that
while the American is disposed to make up the tale
of his profits by sharp bargains, the Scotch are as
much disposed to make it up by liberal treatment of
the land. Why is this? The American is not illib-
eral by nature; a thousand proofs lie to the contrary;
but by an unfortunate traditional belief he is disposed
to count the land only a rigorous step-dame from
which all possible benefit is to be wrested, and the
least possible return made.

Is the Congressional grant for agricultural colleges

to work a change in this belief in the minds of those who hold the great mass of the land under control? Not surely until the newly started colleges shall have made some more vigorous practical demonstration than they have made thus far. The bearings of science upon agriculture were well taught previously under the wing of the established universities; what the public had reason to hope from the new endowment was such practical exhibit of the economic value of a thorough system in tillage and management, as should carry conviction to the popular mind. As yet we wait in vain. Looking at results thus far, I am strongly of the opinion that a few thousands devoted to the gratuitous distribution of one or two sterling agricultural newspapers would have worked more good to the farming interests of the community, than the millions which have been committed to the wisdom of the several State legislatures. I have no hope that these views will meet the concurrence of those who have present control of the funds; nor do I mean to express a doubt of the honesty and good intentions of those who have become the supervisors of this great trust; but I am strongly of the assurance that the common sense of the country is largely disposed to ask of the scientific gentlemen who have been so largely the recipients of this congressional bounty some practical demonstration upon the land, of the faith they hold and teach.

I come back to the old farm, with its meagre stock and its wide acres. Of course there was something to be sold. Farmers never get on without that. First of all, came the " veals "—selling in that day for some two cents a pound, live weight. (They now sell in the New York market for ten.) This bridged over the spring costs, until the butter came from the first growth of the pastures.

—How well I remember tossing myself from bed at an hour before daylight, Seth (by previous orders) having the horse and wagon ready, and by candle-light seeing to the packing of the spring butter—the firkins being enwrapped in dewy grass, fresh cut— and then setting forth upon the long drive (twelve miles) to the nearest market town. What a drive it was! Five miles on, I saw the early people stirring and staring at me, as they washed their faces in the basin at the well. Then came woods, and silence, but a strange odorous freshness in the air—possibly some near coal-pit gave its kreosotic fumes, not unpleasant ; some owl, in the swamps I passed, lifted its melancholy hoot ; further on I saw some early riser driving his cows to pasture ; still further I caught sight of children at play before some farm-house door, and the sun being fairly risen, I knew their breakfasts were waiting them within.

After this, I passed occasional teams upon the

road, and gave a "good morning" to the drivers. Then came the toll-gate: I wondered if the day's profits would be equal to the toll? After this came the milk wagons whisking by me, and I envied them their short rounds; at last (the sun being now two hours high) came sight of the market town—city, I should say; for the legislature had given it long before the benefit of the title; and on the score of church spires, and taverns, and shops, and news-papers, and wickedness, it deserved the name.

I wish I could catch sight once more of the old gentleman (a good grocer as the times went) who plunged his thumb-nails into my golden rolls of but-ter, and said: "We're buying pooty fair butter at twelve and a half cents, but seein' as it's you, we'll say thirteen cents a pound for this," and he cleaned his thumb-nail upon the breech of his trowsers.

I am not romancing here, I am only telling a plain, straightforward story of my advent, some twenty years ago, upon a summer's morning into the city of N—. I recall now vividly the detestably narrow and muddy streets—the poor horse, (I had bought it of the son of our deacon,) wheezing with his twelve-mile drive—my own empty faint stomach —the glimpses of the beautiful river between the hills—and the golden butter which I must needs sell to my friend the grocer at thirteen cents! I hope he had never any qualms of conscience; but it is a faint hope to entertain of grocers. I knew a single naively honest one; but to him I never offered anything for sale. I feared he might succumb to that temptation.

After the butter, (counting some forty odd pounds in weight per week,) the next most important sale was that of the lambs and wool. The lambs counted ordinarily—leaving out the losses of the newly dropped ones by crows * and foxes—some hundred or more. And nice lambs they were; far better than the half I find in the markets to-day. Nothing puts sweeter and more delicate flesh upon young lambs than that luxuriant growth of herbage which springs from freshly cleared high-lying wood-lands. In piquancy and richness, it is as much beyond the lambs of stall-fed sheep, as the racy mutton of the Dartmoors is beyond the turnip-fatted wethers of the downs of Hampshire. And yet these lambs were delivered to the butcher at an ignoble price; I think a dollar and a half a head was all that could be secured for animals which in

---

* Enthusiastic bird-lovers will learn, may be with surprise, that crows are capable of this mischief, but it is even true. Their villainous method is to pluck out the eyes of the newly born innocents, and then leave their prey until death and putrefaction shall have ripened it to their taste. Only extreme hunger, however, will drive the crow to such game. I think I have never felt more murderously inclined than when I have seen upon a bleak day of April one of these black harpies perched upon the head of its faintly struggling victim, and deliberately plucking away the eyes from the socket.

the city would bring to-day nearly five dollars. The wool was bought up by speculators in that time, and the speculators were not extravagant. I remember very well driving off upon a summer's afternoon, mounted upon twelve great sacks of fleeces, and being rather proud of my receipts, at the rate of twenty-eight cents per pound. (The same wool would have brought two years since eighty cents per pound.)

After we disposed of the butter and the wool, and during the late autumn months, came the cartage of wood—some eight miles—to a port upon the river, at which four dollars per cord was paid for good oak wood, and five for hickory. At present rates of labor, these are sums which would not pay for the cutting and cartage.

I must not forget the swine—two or three venerable porkers, and in an adjoining pen a brood of young shoats—that would equip themselves in great layers of fat, from the whey during the hot months, and the yellow ears of corn with the first harvesting of October. Day after day, through May, through June, came the unwearied round of milking, of driving to pasture, of plowing, of planting; day after day the sun beat hotter on the meadows, on the plowland, on the reeking sty; day after day the buds unfolded—the pink of orchards hung in flowery sheets over the scattered apple trees; the dogwood threw

out its snowy burden of blossoms from the edges of
the wood ; the oaks showed their velvety tufts, and
with midsummer there was a world of green and of
silence—broken only by an occasional " Gee, Bright ! "
of the teamster, or the cluck of a matronly hen, or
hum of bees, or the murmur of the brook. All this
inviting to a very dreamy indolence, which, I must
confess, was somehow vastly enjoyable.

Nothing to see ? Lo, the play of light and shade
over the distant hills, or the wind, making tossed and
streaming wavelets on the rye. Nothing to hear ?
Wait a moment and you shall listen to the bursting
melodious roundelay of the merriest singer upon
earth—the black and white coated Bob-o'-Lincoln, as
he rises on easy wing, floats in the sunshine, and
overflows with song, then sinks, as if exhausted by
his brilliant solo, to some swaying twig of the alder
bushes. Nothing to hope ? The maize leaves through
all their close serried ranks are rustling with the
promise of golden corn. Nothing to conquer ? There
are the brambles, the roughnesses, the inequalities,
the chill damp earth, the whole teeming swamp-land.

I have tried to outline the surroundings and appointments of many a back country farmer of New
England to-day. I am sure the drawing is true,
because it is from the life. I seem to see such an one
now on one of these May mornings an hour before

sunrise. It is his market day, and the old sorrel mare is harnessed, and tied to the hitch-post. The wagon is of antique shape, bulging out in front and rear, and with half-rounded ends. The high-backed seat is supported upon a V-shaped framework of ash, and covered over with a yellow buffalo skin, of which the fur is half worn away. An oaken firkin is presently lifted in, with a white linen cloth shut down under its cover, and a corner of the buffalo turned over it to shield it from the dust and the sunshine. Then comes a bushel basket of eggs, packed in rowen hay; next the great clothes-basket, covered with a table cloth, in which lie the two hind quarters of a veal killed yesterday, (the fore quarters being kept for home consumption.) In the corner of the wagon is thrust a squat jug—its stopper being a corn-cob wrapped around with newspaper—which is to be filled with "Port o' reek" molasses. Then, at last, Jerusha, the wife, in silver spectacles, and Sunday gown, clambers in—a stout woman, with her waist belted in, after a loose sausage-like way—who has a last word for her 'darter' Sally Ann, and then another last word, and who cautions Enos (her husband) about "turnin' too short," and who asks if the mare "an't gittin' kind o' frisky with the spring weather?"

So they drive away—Enos and Jerushy. They

talk of the new " howsen " along the way ; they discuss the last Sunday's sermon : Enos says, " I've
heerd that Hosea Wood is a cortin' Malviny Smith."

" Don't b'lieve a word on't, Enos. No sich a
thing. Did you put a baitin' for the hoss in the
waggin, Enos ? "

" No, I vum ! I forgot it," says Enos.

" What a plaguey careless creeter you're a gittin'
to be, Enos ! "

And so the good worthy couple jog on. In town,
the jug is filled ; the stout matron peers through her
spectacles at tapes, thread, needles, and a stout " cal-
iker " gown (fast colors) for Sally Ann. *Pater-fami-
lias* sees to the filling of the flat jug, he makes a fair
sale of the two quarters of veal, he buys a few " gard-
ing " seeds, a new rake, a scythe snathe, and dickers
for a grindstone—unavailingly. Two hours before
nightfall, the good couple jog homeward again, with
humdrum quietude.

It is not such a scene of domesticity as I ever
forecast for my own enjoyment. I believed, and still
believe, that the dead life upon the back country
New England farms, is capable of being stirred into
a live life. Over and over I forecast the day when
the inequalities should be smoothed, the swamps
drained, the woodlands cleared up, (leaving only here
and there some clump of giant oaks or chestnuts

about a loitering brooklet,) the cattle quadrupled in
number, the muck-lands yielding their harvests to be
composted with the concentrated manures of the
town, the very walls to be straightened (of which a
beginning had been made), and such stir and movement and growth and cumulative fertility as should
make the neighborhood open its eyes wide, and stare
to a purpose. I saw the wasting rivulets dammed
and distributing their fertilizing flow over acres of
the side-land; I saw the maple swamps giving place
to wide stretches of heavy meadow; I saw the wild
growth of the pasture-lands cut and piled and burned,
and all the hillsides glittering with a new wealth of
green.

But it was not to be. In the very heat of the
endeavor, there came a flattering invitation to change
the scene of labor and of observation, a single night
only being given for decision. I remember the night
as if only this morning's sun broke it, and kindled it
into day. One way, the brooks, the oaks, the crops,
the memories, the homely hopes, lured me; the other
way, I saw splendid and enticing phantasmagoria—
London Bridge, St. Paul's, Prince Hal, Fleet Street,
Bolt Court, Kenilworth, wild ruins. Next morning
I gave the key of the corn-crib to the foreman, and
bade the farm-land adieu.

Within a month I was strolling over the fields of

Lancashire, wondering at that orderly, systematic cultivation of which New England had not dreamed —wondering at the grand results of this liberal and generous culture, and more than ever disgusted at the pinched and starveling way in which my countrymen were cheating the land of its opulent privilege of production.

I have written this little descriptive episode of a farm-life in New England to serve as the background for certain illustrative hints toward the amendment of rural life—whether in matters of good husbandry, or of good taste ; I have furthermore ventured upon certain homeliness of detail in these opening pages, to show that I may have privilege of speech.

There is no manner of work done upon a New England farm to which some day I have not put my hand—whether it be chopping wood, laying wall, sodding a coal-pit, cradling oats, weeding corn, shearing sheep, or sowing turnips. Therefore, in any future references which I may make in the course of these papers to farm life, I trust that my good readers will credit me with a certain *connaissance de cause.*

ADVICE FOR LACKLAND.

II.

ADVICE FOR LACKLAND.

Pomologists and Common People.

I DO not know that the Horticulturists proper are the best advisers of a man who wishes—as so many do in these times—to establish his little home in the country, and to make it charming with fruits and flowers, and all manner of green things. I think that the professional tastes or successes of one devoted to Horticulture might lead him into a great many extravagances of suggestion, in the entertainment of which, the plain country liver—making lamentable failures—would lose courage and faith. The Pomologists may indeed say that there is no reason to make failure if their suggestions are followed to the letter, and the proper amount of care bestowed. This may be very true; but they do not enough consider that nine out of ten who love the country, and its delights of garden

2

or orchard, can never be brought to that care and nicety of observation, which, with the devoted Horticulturist, is a second nature.

Most men go to the country to make an easy thing of it. If they must commence study of all the later discoveries in vegetable physiology, and keep a sharp eye upon all new varieties of fruit—lest they fall behind the age ; and trench their land every third year, and screen it—may be—in order to ensure the most perfect comminution of the soil, they find themselves entering upon the labors of a new profession, instead of lightening the fatigues of an old one. Any thorough practice of Horticulture does indeed involve all this ; but there are plenty of outsiders, who, without any strong ambition in that direction, have yet a very determined wish to reap what pleasures they can out of a country life, by such moderate degree of attention and of labor as shall not overtax their time, or plunge them into the anxieties of a new and engrossing pursuit.

What shall be done for them ? To talk to such people—and I dare say scores of them may be reading these pages now—about the comparative vigor of a vine grown from a single eye, or a vine grown from a layer, or about the shades of difference in flavor between a Vicomtesse berry and a Triomphe de Gand— is to talk Greek to them ; it is as if a druggist were

to talk about the comparative influences of potash or
of some simple styptic upon an irritated mucous
membrane, to a man who wants simply—something
to cure a sore throat. It is the aim of the Horticulturist to push both land and plants to the last limit
of their capacity—to establish new varieties—to pro-
voke nature by incessant pinchings into some abnor-
mal development ; whereas the aim of the mass of
suburban residents is to have a cheery array of flowers
—good fruit and plenty of it, at the smallest possible
cost. If indeed the latter have any hope of winning
what they wish, by simple transfer of their home
from city to country, without any care or cost whatever, they are grossly mistaken. If a mere, bald love
of fruit-eating, without any love for the means of its
production—calls a man to the country, I would
strongly advise him to stay in town, and buy fruit
at the city markets ; and the man who goes into the
country merely to stretch his legs, I would as strongly
advise to do it on Broadway, or in bed. Nature is a
mistress that must be wooed with a will ; and there
is no mistress worth the having, that must not be
wooed in the same way.

But the distinction remains which I have laid
down between the aims of the Pomologists and of the
quiet country liver. And I am strongly inclined to
think that the former are a little too much disposed

to sneer at the simple tastes of the latter. There is a
sturdy professional pride that enters into this, for
something. I have before now been thrown into the
company of breeders of blooded stock who would not
so much as notice the best native animals—no matter
how tenderly cared for, or how assiduously combed
down; and yet a good dish of cream most people
relish, even if the name of the cow is not written in
the Herd-books. Of course that nice discrimination
of tastes which enables a man to detect the minute
shades of difference in flavors, is a thing of growth
and long culture, and every man is inclined to respect
what has cost him long culture. But if I smack my
lips over the old Hovey, or a mahogany colored Wil-
son, and stick by them, I do not know that the zealous Pomologist has a right to condemn me utterly,
because I do not root up my strawberry patches and
plant Russell's Prolific, or the Jocunda in their place.
It is even doubtful if extreme cultivation of taste does
not do away with a great deal of that hearty gusto
with which most men enjoy good fruit. The man
who is all the summer through turning some little
tid-bit of flavor upon the tip of his tongue, and going
off into fits of rumination upon the possible difference
of flavor between a Crimson-Cone when watered from
an oak tub, and a Crimson-Cone when watered from
a chestnut tub, seems to me in a fair way of losing all

the appreciable and honest enjoyment of fruit which he ever had in his life. There lives about the London-Dock-Vaults a race of pimpled-faced men whose professional service it is to guzzle small draughts of Chateaux Margaux or of rare Port, which they whip about with their tongues and expend their tasting faculties upon, with enormous gravity : but who in the world supposes that these can have the same appreciation of an honest bumper of wine, which a quiet Christian gentleman has, who sits down to his dinner with a moderate glass of good, sound Bordeaux at his elbow ?

Outsiders may, I think, find a little comfort in this, and take courage in respect of their old Hovey patches—if they will keep them only clean and rich.

But I have not said all this out of any want of regard for Horticulture as an art, demanding both skill and devotion ; nor have I said it from any want of respect for those pomologists who are boldly leading the van in the prosecution of the Art ; but I have wished simply to clear away a little platform from which to talk about the wants of humble cultivators, and the way in which those wants are to be met.

And here my old question recurs—what shall be done for them ?

To give my reply definite shape, I picture to myself my old friend Lackland, who has grown tired of thumping over the city pavements, who has two or three young children to whom he wishes to give a free tumble on the green sward, and who has an intense desire to pick his grapes off his own vine, instead of buying them on Broadway at forty cents the pound. He comes to me for advice.

"My dear fellow," I should say, "there's no giving any intelligible advice to a man whose notions are so crude. Do you want a country home for the year, or only a half home for six months in the year, from which you'll be flitting when the leaves are gone?"

"To be sure," says he, "it's worth considering. And yet what difference could it make with your suggestions? Once established, I could determine better."

"It makes this difference:—if you propose to establish a permanent home for the year, you want to provide against wintry blasts; you don't want a hilltop where a northwester will be driving in your teeth all November; you want shelter; and you want near walks for your children through the snow-banks to school or church; and you don't want the sea booming at the foot of your garden all winter long. If it's only a summer stopping place you have your eye upon, all these matters are of little account."

"Suppose we make it a permanent home," says

Lackland, "how much ground do I want to grow all
the fruit and vegetables I may need for my family?"

"That depends altogether upon your mode of
culture. If you mean to trench and manure thoroughly, and have good soil to start with, and keep it up
to the best possible condition, a half acre will more
than supply you."

"Call it two acres," says he, "and what shall I
plant upon it?"

What shall a man plant upon his two acres of
ground, on which he wishes to establish a cozy home,
where his children can romp to their hearts' content,
and he—take a serene pleasure in plucking his own
fruit, pulling his own vegetables, smelling at his own
rose-tree and smoking under his own vine? If he
goes up with the question to some high court of Horticulture, he comes away with a list as long as my
arm—in which are *remontants* that must be strawed
over, vines that must be laid down, vegetables that
must be coaxed by a fortnight of forcing, rare shrubs
that must have their monthly pinching, monster berries that must have their semi-weekly swash of guano
water, and companies of rare bulbs that, after wilting
of the leaves, must be dug, and dried, and watched,
and put out of reach, and found again, and replanted.

And my friend Lackland reporting such a list to
me, sees a broad grin gradually spreading over my face.

" You think it a poor list, then ? " says he.

" I beg your pardon; it's a most capital one; there are the newest things of every sort in it; and if you cultivate them as they ought to be cultivated, you'll make a fine show; they'll elect you member of a Horticultural Society; heaven only knows but they'll name you on a tasting committee."

" That would be jolly," says he.

" And you'll need plenty of bass-matting, and patent labels, and lead wire, and a box of grafting instruments, and brass syringes of different capacities, and gauze netting for some of your more delicate fruits, and porcelain saucers to float your big gooseberries in, and forcing beds, and guano tanks, and a small propagating house, and a padlock on your garden, and a Scotchman to keep the key at seventy dollars a month, and a fag to work the compost-heaps at forty-five more."

" The devil I will ! " he says.

" Don't be profane," I should say, " or if you needs must, you'll have better occasion for it when you get fairly into the traces."

And then—more seriously—" My dear fellow, the list, as I have said, is a capital one; but it supposes most careful culture, extreme attention, and a love for all the niceties of the art—which you have not got. You want to take things easy; you don't want to torment yourself with the idea that your children may be plucking unaware your specimen berries; you don't want to lock them out of the garden. As sure as you undertake such a venture you'll be at odds with your Scotchman; you'll lose the names of your own trees; you'll forget the hyacinths; your 'half-hardys' will all be scotched by the second winter; your dwarf 'Vicars' that need such careful nursing and high dressing will dwindle into lean shanks of pears that have no flavor. My advice to you is—to throw the fine list in the fire; to limit yourself, until you have felt your way, to some ten or a dozen of the best established varieties; don't be afraid of old things if they are good; if a gaunt Rhode Island Greening tree is struggling in your hedge-row, trim it, scrape it, soap it, dig about it, pull away the turf from it, lime it, and then if you can keep up a fair fight against the bugs and the worms, you will have fine fruit from it; if you can't, cut it down. If a veteran mossy pear tree is in your door-yard, groom it as you would a horse—just in from a summering in briary pastures—put scions of Bartlett, of Winter Nelis, of Rostiezer into its top and sides. In an unctuous spot of your garden, plant your dwarf Duchess, Bonne de Jersey, Beurre Diel, and your Glout Morceau. If either don't do well, pull it up and burn it; don't waste labor on a sickly young

2*

tree. Save some sheltered spot for a trellis, where you may plant a Delaware, an Iona or two, a Rebecca, and a Diana. Put a Concord at your south-side door—its rampant growth will cover your trellised porch in a pair of seasons : it will give you some fine clusters, even though you allow it to tangle : the pomologists will laugh at you ; but let them : you will have your shade and the wilderness of frolicsome tendrils, and at least a fair show of purple bunches. Scatter here and there hardy herbaceous flowers that shall care for themselves, and which the children may pluck with a will. Don't distress yourself if your half acre of lawn shows some hummocks, or dandelions, or butter-cups. And if a wild clump of bushes intrude in a corner, don't condemn it too hastily ; it may be well to enliven it with an evergreen or two—to dig about it, and paint its edges with a few summer phloxes or roses. You will want neither Scotchman nor forcing houses for this."

This is the way in which I should have talked to my friend Lackland, who would want to take things easy.

I should not wonder if he were to buy his place of two acres, and make trial. God bless him if he does.

Lackland Makes a Beginning.

MY friend Lackland—as I suspected he would—
has purchased a little place of two and a half
acres, some thirty or forty miles from the city by the
New Haven railway. He makes his trips to and
fro with a little badly-disguised fear of decayed
" sleepers," it is true ; and suffers from the still more
frequent embarrassment of riding upon his feet—all
the seats being occupied, and the company being
unfortunately too much straitened in their circumstances to add to the number of their carriages.
He was disposed to resent such things at the start,
and was even stirred into writing a brief and indig-
nant appeal to an independent morning journal ; but
upon being answered by an attorney for the company
or a road commissioner, who called him names and
abused him, as if he had been a witness before a
court of justice, he subsided into that meek respect
for corporations, and awe of all their procedure,
which are the characteristics of a good American
citizen, and of most well-ordered newspapers.

New Yorkers learn how to bear such things ;
there is no better schooling for submission than a
two or three years course of travel upon the city
railways ; Lackland is submissive. And after a

fatiguing day in Maiden Lane, having come up
Fourth Avenue with a stout woman in his lap, he
is grateful for even a standpoint upon one of the
New Haven cars.

But this is all by the way.

My friend Lackland has, as I said, bought a small
country place within a mile of village and station,
for which the purchase-money, in round numbers, was
six thousand dollars. A certain proportion of this
sum was paid in view of a projected horse railway,
which is to pass the door, and to unfold building
sites over his whole area of land. As yet, however,
it is in the rough. There is indeed "a brand-new
house upon it—two stories, and only three years
built," as he writes me, "with ell wash-room, and
all well painted with two coats of white lead. The
property is distributed into six different enclosures,
of which I send you a draught."

And herewith I give the exhibit of Mr. Lackland's little place, with its condition at time of purchase.

"You will observe," he continues, "that there is
rather a cramped aspect about the door-yard and
entrance, these being hemmed in by a white picket
fence on either side and in front. It is unfortunately
the only sound fence about the premises; the garden
(c) showing a tottering remnant of one of the same

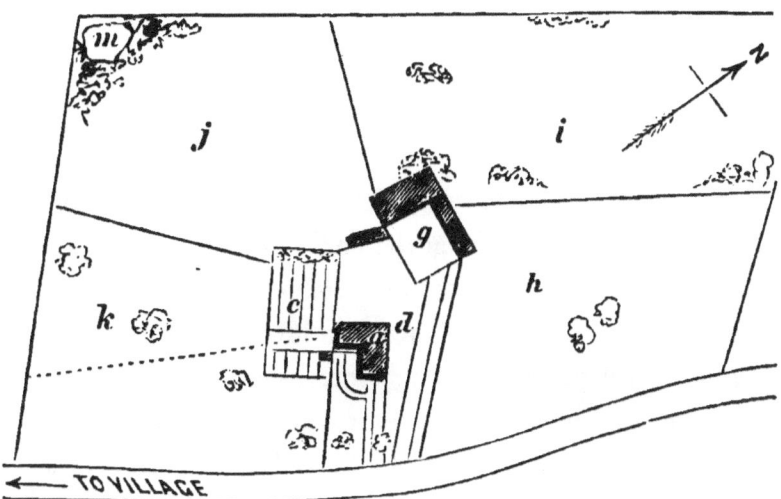

← TO VILLAGE

pattern, and the other enclosures never having boasted anything finer than 'post and rail' fixtures, with a half-wall to prop them upon some of the exterior lines. The enclosure (*d*) is what the previous owner called his back yard; it was traversed, as you see, by a cart-path leading straight to the barn court, and was encumbered with a prodigious array of old wood, brush heaps, a broken cart or two, and one of the most luxurious thickets of burdock and stramonium which I ever remember to have seen. He (former owner) tells me stramonium is good for 'biles.' Is it?

"The buildings around the little enclosure marked (*g*) will explain themselves—a barn, a hog-pen, a cow-shed—all in most dilapidated condition, so much so that I shall have to make a new investment in the way of stable room. There is the remnant of an old orchard upon the plot marked (*k*), with only three or four ragged and disorderly looking trees; at (*j*) again, there is a patch which has been in potatoes and corn for an indefinite number of years, and which has a terrible bit of ledge in the corner (marked *m*) over-run with briars and stunted cedars, that I fear will cost a round sum to reduce to a level. The fields (*i*) and (*h*) are pieces of mangy grass scattered over with occasional bushes, but I do not despair of putting a smooth face upon them. The only view from the premises that is worth considering, is rather a pretty one (indicated by a dotted line) of the village spire, and a few of the village roofs peeping out from the trees, and back of them a glimpse of the Sound. I send a rough sketch of it.

"But the misfortune is, the view is only to be seen to advantage from my wash-room door, or from one spot in the garden just now encumbered with enormous Lawton briars. The first position is soapy and damp for visitors, and the last—tedious.

"What I wish of you,"—my friend Lackland continues to write,—"is to give me a hint or two about the combing of this rough little home of mine into shape. And in order to a more definite understanding I will tell you briefly what I *don't* want, and next what I *do* want.

"And first, being a plain man, I don't want crooked walks, for the mere sake of having them crooked; I don't want to go into my gate in a hurry —when I know dinner is already smoking on the table—and yet, after entrance, be compelled to describe a circle planted with I know not what barbarian evergreens, before I can get to my door.

"I don't want my stable yard absolutely in sight; least of all do I wish to be compelled to traverse it, before I can get sight of my pet mare.

"I don't wish a carriage drive to my door-step, when my door is only fifty feet from the road by a tape-line.

"I don't want to pull down or to move the present house, because in so doing I should sacrifice a capital

cellar, which I must do the previous owner the justice
to say, has been capitally arranged.

"I don't want such a great array of fences; I
don't want a labyrinth of walks; I don't want my
garden so near the street as that chance passers-by
shall see me in my shirt sleeves and hail me with:
Hello! Squire, what you goin' to ask a peck for them
pa'snips ?'

"I *do* want a little of good elbow-room about the
house and entrance, as if I were not in momentary
fear of an incursion of pigs from the back yard; I do
want a garden of somewhat larger area, where I can
grub away at my will; and if you draw me a plan,
put at least a fourth of the whole land into herbs and
garden stuff. I want the view kept of the village
spire, and the background of sea, and some lounging
place from which I may look upon it at my leisure.
I want a poultry-yard of such dimensions that I may
count upon a fresh egg every day to my breakfast; I
want provision for a salad on Easter Sunday; and if
you could contrive me some cheap fashion of a cold
grapery to try my hand upon, I should be thankful;
only let it be so situated that I may (if grapes fail)
turn it into a winter room for my hens. I want you
to tell me what I can do with the rock I must blast
away from the edge in the corner of the potatoe-
patch. I want something I may call a lawn—to

satisfy my wife's pride—and a bit or two of shrubbery in it. But above all, I want at least a third of
the land in good wholesome greensward, with no
encumbering trees—whether fruit or exotic—where I
may turn my mare for a run, or play at base ball with
my boys, or cut a bit of hay, or—if the humor takes
me—try my hand at a premium crop of something."

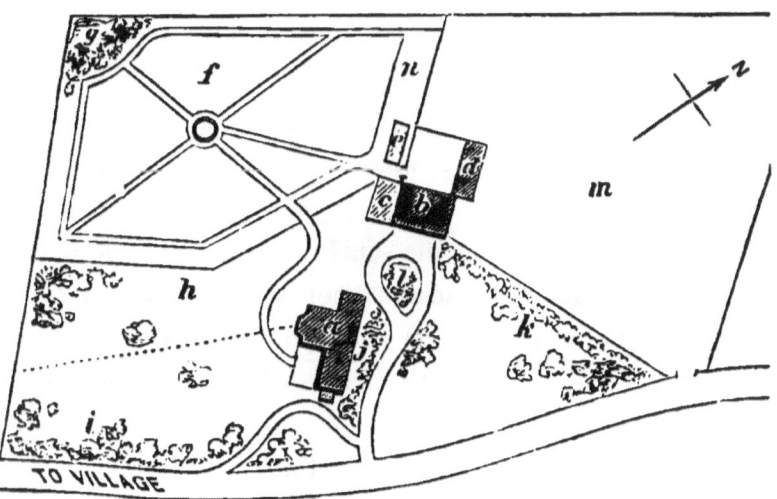

Upon this I made a little study of Lackland's plot
of land, and furnished him with this design.

And I furthermore said to him, your ledge (which
I have marked *g*) is one of the most picturesque
features about your place; so I have thrown it boldly
into your garden, in such way that it will be in full
view from the gate, and I advise you to cherish it—

to plant columbines on its ledges, and your Tom
Thumb geraniums along its lower edge, in such sort
that in autumn they will seem like a running flame
of fire skirting the cliff and blending with the crimson
verbenas upon the circle in the centre of the garden.
In (*f*) you have a map of the garden and your work
place, and to make the privacy of it entire, you may
plant a hedge for a barrier along the line (*h*) or you
may set a trellis there and cover it with vines. At
(*e*) you have a hot-bed to provide your Easter salad,
and you may multiply the hot-beds if you like along
the border (*n*) which is made under shelter of a high
fence to the north. At (*c*) you have your cheap
grapery built against the south-side of the barn, and
convenient for the transmutation you suggest; at (*b*)
is your stable, and at (*d*) your poultry house with a
sunny stable court to the south of it. At (*m*) you
have your paddock for the mare, or your mall for
base-ball, or your plow-ground for a premium crop—
utterly free from shrubbery, and communicating with
barn and with street alike. The lawn explains and
describes itself; but I would only suggest that the
shrubbery marked (*j*) will be a capital spot, under
shade from south, for your Rhododendrons; * and the

---

* Various horticulturists have discussed the method of isolating
a border of rhododendrons from the influences of a forest screen to
the south—one suggesting simple amputation of the roots of the

circle (*l*) I would advise you to fill with a dense coppice of hemlock spruce to break the wind from the north. Along the border marked (*k*) you can either plant apple trees, and at fifteen feet of distance, a thicker line of dwarf pears (being careful to trench or subsoil the ground), or you can stock it with a protecting belt of evergreens. In either case, give thorough cultivation, if you wish the best results.

At (*a*) is the " brand-new " house remodelled in such fashion that you have a southern porch, a kitchen in the rear, and a bay-window in your dining-room, which commands (by the dotted line) the same view which now wastes its charm upon the stout woman at your wash-tub.

It is possible that my friend Lackland may report progress to me some time in the course of the summer.

trees forming the screen, and the other the interposition of a wall. The last is expensive and the former liable to be neglected. An open ditch, some two feet deep by eighteen inches wide, I have seen most effectively employed for the end proposed, by a very successful southern horticulturist, who succeeded, year after year, in securing a magnificent bloom of some ten or twelve varieties of Azaleas, within twenty feet of gigantic cypresses and magnolias. The ditch may also serve as a convenient receptacle for leaves and the rakings of the borders.

Lackland's House Plans.

UNFORTUNATELY, almost every city gentleman who comes into possession—whether by
purchase or otherwise—of a plain country house,
from which some honest well-to-do farmer has just
decamped, puzzles his brain first of all, to know how
he shall make a "fine thing" of it. My advice to
such puzzled gentlemen, in nine cases out of ten,
would be—" not to do it."

If the ceilings are low, and the beams show here
and there the generous breadth and depth of timber
which old-time builders put into their frames, cherish
these remembrances of a sturdier stock than ours;
scrub and paint and paper as you will, but if the
skeleton be stanch, and no dry rot shake the joints
or give a sway to the floors and ceiling—try, for a
few years at least, the moral effect of an old house.
It can do no harm to a dapper man from the city. It
may teach his wife possibly some of the humilities
which she cannot learn on Broadway. With a free,
bracing air whistling around the house corners, and
here and there an open fire within, low rooms are by
no means poisonous; and if the trees do not so far
shade the roof as to keep away the fierce outpourings
of a summer's sun, and the low chambers carry a

stifling air in August, it is only necessary, in many
instances, to tear away the garret flooring, and to run
up the chamber ceilings into tent-like canopies, with
a ventilator in their peak—to have as free circulation
as in the town attics. And such tented ceilings may
be prettily hung with French striped papers, with a
fringe-like border at the line of junction of the verti-
cal with the sloping wall—in such sort that your
military friend, if he comes to pass a July night with
you, may wake with the illusion of the camp upon
him, and listen to such *réveille* as the crowing of a
cock, or the piping of a wren.

But a monstrous and intolerable grievance to all
people of taste lies in the attempt to set off one of
those grave exteriors, at which I have hinted, by
some of the more current architectural cockneyisms.
Thus, an ancient door, with the dark green paint in
blisters upon it, and opening in the middle, perhaps,
is torn away to give place to the newest fancy from
the sash factories, and a glazing of red and blue.
For my part, I have great respect for a door that has
banged back and forth its welcomes and its good-
byes for half a century; the very blisters on it seem to
me only the exuding humors of a jovial hospitality;
and all the weather-stains are but honorable scars of
a host of battles against wind and rain. I would no
more barter such an old-time door against the new-

ness of the joiners, than I would barter old-time honesty against that of Oil Creek, or of Wall Street.

Then again, your cockney must tear away the homely sheltering porch, with its plank "settles" on either side, for some stupendous affair, with columns for which all heathenism has been sacked to supply the capitals.

If renovation must be made, it should be made in keeping with the original style of the house—except indeed change go so far as to divest it altogether of the old aspect. In some farm-houses that may be taken in hand for repairs, it might be well even to strain a point in the direction of antiquity, and to replace a swagging door by a stanch one of double-battened oak or chestnut, with its wrought nails showing their heads in checkered diamond lines up and down, and its hinges, worked into some fanciful pattern of a dragon's tail, exposed. Then there should be a ponderous iron knocker, whose din should reach all over the house, and the iron thumb-latch—not cast and japanned, but showing stroke of the hammer, and taking on rust where the maid cannot reach with her brick-dust. Of course, too, there should be the two diamond lights like two great eyes peering from under the frontlet of the old-fashioned stoop. All these, if the house be so ancient and weather-stained as to admit of it, will demonstrate that the occupant

is among the few who are left in these days of petroleum, who make a merit of homeliness, and cherish
tenderly its simplest features. If the house be really
weak in the joints, the sooner it comes down the
better ; but if it has snugness and stiffness and comfort, let not the owner be persuaded of the carpenters
to graft upon it the modernisms of their tricksy
joinery. I can well understand how a dashing buck
of two or three and thirty should prefer a young
woman in her furbelows, to an old one in her bomb-
azine ; but if the fates put him in leash with an
ancient lady, let him think twice before he bedizens
her gray head with preposterous frontlets, and puts a
mesh of girl's curls upon the nape of her old neck.

I have said all this as a prelude to a little talk
about certain changes which my friend Lackland has
wrought in his country place—thirty miles away by
the New Haven road. The house he purchased could
boast no respectability of age. The height of its
rooms was of that medium degree which neither suggested any notion of quaintness nor of airiness. Its
entrance-hall was pinched and narrow ; its stairway
inhospitably lean, and altogether its appointments
had that cribbed and confined aspect, which, to one
used to width and sunshine, was almost revolting.
The wash-room was positively the only apartment
below stairs which had a southern aspect. I give his

drawing of it, and it is a good type of a great many
"small and convenient houses" scattered through our
country towns.

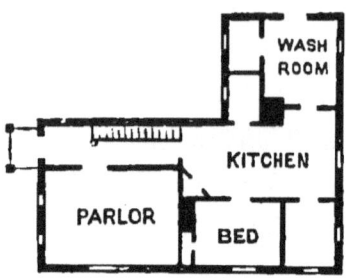

"Of course, this will never do," wrote Lackland
to me, "and yet the skin of the house (as our carpenter calls it) is very good, and I wish to make the
needed changes, so far as possible, without disturbing
the exterior outline of the main building. But how
shall I rid myself of that preposterously narrow entrance-way in which I can almost fancy Mrs. L., (who
is something large) getting wedged on some warm
day? How shall I throw sunlight into that dismal
parlor? You will perceive that along the whole
south front there is not a single available window
below. Now, half the charm of a country place, to
my notion, lies in the possession of some sunny porch
upon which the early vines will clamber, and under
whose eaves the Phœbe birds will make their nests.

I want, too, my after-dinner lounges at a sunny door, where I can smoke my pipe, basking in the yellow light, as I watch the shadows chasing over the grass. About the stupid little design I send you, there is neither hope nor possibility of this.

"Again, even with a dining-room, or library added, and perhaps a kitchen, I shall be still in want of further chamber range, which if I gain (as our carpenter suggests) by piling on a story more, it appears to me that I should give to' the narrow front of the house an absurd cock-loft look that would be unendurable.

"Mrs. L. and myself have scored out an incredible number of diagrams—all which have been discussed, slept on, admired, and eventually condemned. Sometimes it is the old pinched entrance way that works

3

condemnation; sometimes (on my part) the lack of sunny exposure; and oftenest (on hers) the lack of closets. She insists that no man yet ever planned a house properly on this score. She doesn't see clearly (being deficient in mathematics) why a closet shouldn't be made in every partition wall. She don't definitely understand, I think, why a person should thwack his head in a closet under the stairs. She sometimes (our carpenter tells us) insists upon putting a window through a chimney; and on one occasion (it was really a very pretty plan) contrived so as to conduct a chimney through the middle of the best bed room; and the nicest scheme of all, to my thinking, positively had the stairs left out entirely.

"In this dilemma, I want you to tell us what can be done with the old shell, so as to make it passably habitable, until we find out if this new passion for country life is to hold good."

Upon this I ventured to send him this little plan of adaptation, which, though not without a good many faults that could be obviated in building anew, yet promised to meet very many of their wants, and gave to Lackland his sunny frontage.

"Here you have," I wrote him, " your south door, and porch to lounge upon, and your south bow window to your library, which, if the rural tastes grow upon you, you can extend into a conservatory, covering the whole southern flank of the apartment. The parlor, too, has its two south windows, and although

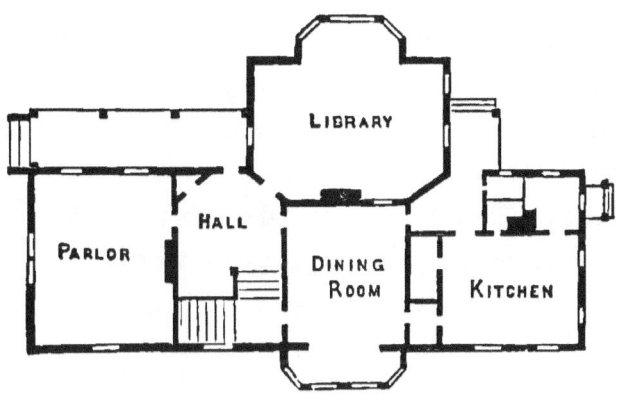

I should have preferred to place the chimney upon the northern side, to the exclusion of the window there, yet it seemed best to make use of the flue already established. The hall is well lighted from the north, and will give room for the hanging of any of your great-aunt's portraits, if you have any.

"There is an objection to traversing the dining-room in going from the kitchen to the hall-door; but it could not well be obviated, with the existing shell of your house, without reducing the size of the dining-room too much, or (another resource) without increasing largely the dimensions of the hall—throwing the intervening space between it and kitchen into store rooms and making the library do duty for the spread of your table.

"The dining-room, moreover, having only north exposure, you may condemn as dismal. I propose to obviate this and to give it a cheerful south light by an extravagance which I dare say the architects will condemn, but which will have its novelty and possible convenience.

"The fireplaces of library and of dining-room, are, you observe, back to back. Now I would suggest that the two flues be carried up with a sweep to either side (uniting in the garret) in such sort, that a broad arched opening shall be left above the mantel from one room into the other. This may be draped, if you like, with some tasteful upholstery; but not so far as to forbid a broad flow of the warm light from the bow window of the library; while upon the mantels of even height, you may place a Wardian case that shall show its delicate plumes of fern between your table and the southern sunlight all winter long. It would moreover be quite possible, owing to the breadth of partition wall afforded by the two flues, to arrange folding shutters for the complete closing of the arch-way whenever desired. For my own part, I love such little novelties of arrangement, which mark a man's house as his own, however much they may put the carpenters to the gape.

"As for the additional chamber-room, never think of putting a third story upon so narrow-throated a house, or you will give it an irredeemable gawkyness. If the space be needed, find it by throwing a mansard roof over all, and lighting your cock-lofts with dormer windows. Then paint with discretion; avoid white, and all shades of lilac—the most abominable color that was ever put upon a house—you can't match the flowers, and don't try, I beg. A mellow brown or a cool gray are the best for the principal surfaces. In

the trimmings, study narrowly the gradients of color. Let there be no forced contrasts, and no indecisive mingling of tones; above all, remember that with your elevations, you want to aim to reduce the apparent height; work in, therefore, as many horizontal lines of decisive color as your exterior carpentry will allow; give dark hoods, if you will, to your front parlor windows, and let the cornice-finish below your mansard roof reach well down, and carry dark shading.

" When you are fairly in, I will come and see how you look."

Lackland's Gardener.

WITH his grounds laid out and his house in fairly habitable condition—according to the plans already laid before the reader—Lackland holds various consultations in regard to a proper gardener —consults as in duty bound, first of all, Mrs. Lackland.

Mrs. Lackland wishes an industrious, sober man, who will keep the walks neat and tidy, who knows enough of flowers not to hoe up any of her choice annuals,—(whose seeds she dots about in all directions, marking the places with fragments of twigs thrust in at all possible angles); she wishes moreover, a good-natured man, who shall be willing to come and pot a flower for her at a moment's notice; one who will not forget the sweet marjoram or the sage, and who will not allow the thyme to die in the winter.

He consults the city seedsmen, who refer him to a half-dozen of stout men who may be lounging upon the barrels in the front of their sales-rooms on almost any fine morning in April; but, on entering into parley with them, he is so confounded with their talk about ranges, and pits, and bottom heat, and Pelargoniums, and Orchids, that he withdraws in disgust.

He consults the newspapers, where he finds a considerable array of advertisements of " steady, capable men, willing to make themselves useful upon a gentleman's place ; " he communicates with some two or three of the most promising advertisers, and arranges for an interview with them. Lackland has great faith, like almost all the men I ever met, in his study of physiognomy. About a man's temper or his honesty, he can hardly be mistaken, he thinks, if he can once set eyes upon him. He is therefore strongly disposed in favor of a stout, jolly-faced Irishman, who assures him he can grow as good " vigitables as enny man in Ameriky."

" And flowers, Patrick (Patrick O'Donohue is his name), you could take care of the flowers ? "

" Oh, flowers, and begorra, yis, sir—roses, pinks, vi'lets—roses—whativer you wish, sir."

2*

"And, Patrick, you could harness a horse some-times if it were necessary."

"Horses, and indade, yis, sir; ye may jist say I'm at home in a stable, sir."

"And the poultry, Patrick, you could look after the poultry, couldn't you?"

"And indade, sir, that's what I can; there's niver a man in the counthry can make hens lay as I can make 'em lay."

In short, Lackland bargains with Patrick, and reports him at the home-quarters "a perfect jewel of a man."

The best of implements are provided, and a great stock of garden seeds—the choice of the latter being determined on after family consultation, in which all the vegetables ever heard of by either party to the counsel, have been added to the list. If a man have a garden, why not enjoy all that a garden can pro-duce—egg-plants, and okra, and globe artichokes, and salsify, and white Naples radishes, and Brussels sprouts? The seed of all these are handed over to the willing Patrick, who, as Mrs. Lackland im-pressively enumerates the different labels (Patrick not being competent to the reading of fine print, as he freely confesses), repeats after her, "Naples radish, yis, m'am; artichokes, yis, m'am; okra, yis, m'am."

Lackland provides frames and glass for the early salads he covets so much, and Patrick, with the fresh sweepings of the stables, has presently a bed all a-steam. At the mere sight of it the Lacklands regale themselves with thoughts of crisp radishes, and the mammoth purple fruit of the egg-plants. The seeds are all put in—early cabbage, cauliflower, peppers, radishes—under the same frame by the judicious O'Donohue. The cabbages and the radishes come forward with a jump. Their expedition forms a pleasant theme for the physiological meditation of Lackland. He is delighted with the stable manure, with the cabbage seed, and with the O'Donohue. He is inclined to think disrespectfully of the seed of peppers and of egg plants in the comparison. But the bland O'Donohue says, " We must give 'em a little more hate."

And after some three or four days, Lackland is stupefied, on one of his visits to his hot bed, to find all his fine radishes and cabbages fairly wilted away; there is nothing left of them but a few sun-blackened stumps; the peppers and egg-plants show no signs of germination.

" What does all this mean ? " says Lackland ; " the cabbages are dead, Patrick."

" Yis, sir—it's the hate, sir. The sun is very strong here, sir ; we must give 'em a little more air, sir."

And they get the air—get the air (by a little for-getfulness on the part of Patrick) night as well as day; the peppers and egg-plants, after a fortnight more of expectation, do not appear.

"How's this, Patrick? no start yet."

"And are ye sure the seed's good, sir?"

"It's all Thorburn's seed."

"Then, of course, it *ought* to be good, sir; but, ye see, there's a dale o' chatery now-a-days, sir."

In short, Lackland's man Patrick is a good-natured blunder-head, who knows no better than to submit his young cauliflowers and peppers to the same atmospheric conditions in the forcing frame. The result is that Lackland buys his first salads in the market, and his first peas in the market, and his first beets in the market. All these creep along very slowly under Patrick's supervision, and the onion seed is fairly past hope, being buried too deep for the sun to have any influence upon its germinating proper-ties.

"But how is this," says the long-suffering Lack-land, at last, "our neighbors are all before us, Pat-rick?"

"Well, sir, it's me opinion that the land is a bit cowld, sir. Wait till July, sir, and you'll see vigi-tables."

And Patrick grubs away with a great deal of

misdirected energy—slicing off, in the heat of his
endeavor, two or three of Mrs. Lackland's choicest
rocket larkspurs; whereupon that lady comes down
upon him with some zeal.

"Larkspur! and that's a larkspur, is it, m'am
(scratching his head reflectingly)? and, begorra, I
niver once thought 'twas a larkspur. Pity, pity; and
so it was, indade, a larkspur? Well, well, but it's
lucky it wa'nt a rose-bush, m'am."

And yet the good-natured blunder-head in the
shape of a gardener is far more endurable, to one
thoroughly interested in country life, than the surly
fellow who, if he gives you early vegetables, resents
a suggestion, and who will take a pride in making
any particular scheme of the proprietor miscarry by
a studied neglect of its details.

Upon the whole, I should lay down as sound
advice for any one who, like Lackland, is beginning
to establish for himself a home in the country that
shall be completely enjoyable, the following rules
with respect to the pursuit and employment of a
gardener:

First, if your notion of country enjoyment is
limited by thought of a good place where you may
lie down under the trees, and frolic with your children, or smoke a pipe under your vine, or clambering
rose-tree at evening—find a gardener who is thorough-

ly taught, and who can place upon your table every day the freshest and crispest of the vegetables and fruits of the season, leaving you no care, but the care of bills for superphosphates and trenching. If you stroll into his domain of the garden, take your walking-stick or your pipe there, if you choose—but never a hoe or a pruning knife. Joke with him, if you like, but never advise him. Take measure of his fitness by the fruits he puts upon your table, the order of your grounds, and the total of your bills. If these are satisfactory—keep him : if not, discharge him, as you would a lawyer who managed your case badly, or a doctor who bled or purged you to a sad state of depletion.

If, on the other hand, in establishing a country home, you have a wish to identify yourself with its growth into fertility and comeliness, in such sort that you may feel that every growing shrub is a little companion for you and yours—every vine a friend— every patch of herbs, of vegetables, or of flowers, an aid to the common weal and pleasures of home, in which you take, and will never cease to take, a personal interest and pride—if all this be true, and you have as good as three hours a day to devote to personal superintendence—then, by all means, forswear all gardeners who come to you with great recommendations of their proficiency. However just these may be, all their accomplishments, ten to one, will be only a grievance to you. It is far better, if you be really in earnest to taste ruralities to the full, to find some honest, industrious fellow—not unwilling to be taught—who will lend a cheerful hand to your efforts to work out the problem of life in the country for yourself.

You will blunder; but in such event you will enjoy the blunders. You will burn your young cabbages, but you will know better another year. Your first grafts will fail, but you will find out why they fail. You will put too much guano to your sweet corn, but you will have a pungent agricultural fact made clear to you. You will leave your turnips and beets standing too thickly in the rows; but you will learn by the best of teaching—never to do so again. You will buy all manner of fertilizing nostrums—and of this it may require a year or two to cure you. You will believe in every new grape, or strawberry, —and of this it may require many years to cure you. You will put faith, at the first, in all the horticultural advices you find in the newspapers,—and of this you will speedily be cured.

In short, whoever is serious about this matter, of taking a home in the country (if his rural taste be a native sentiment, and not a whim), should abjure the presence of a surly master in the shape of a gardener, who can tell him how the Duke of Buccleugh (or any other) managed such matters.

God manages all of nature's growth and bloom in such way, that every earnest man with an observant eye can so far trace the laws of His Providence, as to insure to himself a harvest of fruit, or grain, or flowers. And whatever errors may be made are only so many instructors, to teach, and to quicken love by their lesson.

Let us not then despair of our friend Lackland, though his cabbages are burnt, and his beets are behind the time. I shall visit him again, and trust that I may find his verbenas and lilies in bloom, though his larkspurs have been cut down.

A Pig and a Cow.

I PROPOSE an odd horticultural subject; but the man who plants a garden, and builds a cottage, and carries in his thought the hope of shaking off the dust of the city under green trees upon his own sward-land, where some—nameless party—in white lawn, with blue ribbon of a sash (as in Mr. Irving's pretty picture of a wife), stands ready to greet him, after an hour of torture at the hands of our humane railroad directors—the man, I say, who looks forward to all this, and enters upon the experience, thinks, sooner or later, of a cow and a pig—the pig to consume the waste growth of his garden, and the cow to supply such tender food for his growing ones as they most need.

The pig can hardly be regarded as a classic animal; Virgil, indeed, introduces him as crunching acorns under elm-trees—which account I cannot help reckoning as apocryphal. But he is a very jolly and frisky little animal in his young days, not without a good deal of clumsy grace in his movements, and showing a most human zeal for the full end of the trough.

There is almost the same diversity of opinion with respect to the different races of pigs, which our horticultural friends indulge in with respect to fruits. It is always an awkward matter to discuss the merits of different families, whether of animals who talk, or animals who only grunt or bellow. If the raw suburban resident, in whose interest I make these notes, has an ambition to rear a prize hog that shall outweigh anything his neighbors can show, and intends to keep his bin full of rank material, I should certainly advise the great-boned Chester County race, which, with judicious feeding, come to most elephantine proportions. If, on the other hand, he should prefer a dapper, snug-jointed beast, that shall not be particular in regard to food, and which will yield him cutlets in which the muscular material shall not be utterly overlaid and lost in fatty adipose matter, I should counsel the sleek Berkshire. Or if, uniting the two, he should desire a delicate limbed, well-rounded, contented little animal, that shall browse with equanamity upon the purslane and the spare beet-tops from his garden, I know none safer to commend than the Suffolks. Nor is it essential that he be thorough bred, since the tokens of *pur sang* are a red baldness, and a possible twisting away of the beast's own tail, which do not contribute to good looks.*

All this is but preparatory to my reply to Lack-land, who writes to me: " We have voted to have a pig and a cow; what kinds shall I get, and how shall I keep them, and what shall I do with them ? "

And I wrote back to him: " Buy what the dealers will sell you for a Suffolk; if he lack somewhat in purity of blood (as he probably will), don't be punctilious in the matter. Let his sleeping and eating quarters be high and dry; and if you can manage beyond this a little forage ground for him to disport himself in, and wallow (if he will) on wet days—so much the better. The forage, if you keep him sup-

---

* I must drop, in a note, commendatory mention of the Earl of Sefton Stock, of which a few animals have latterly found their way to this country—a trim, sound, long-bodied breed, easy keepers, and giving, with proper care, delicious rashers of bacon.

plied with raw material in the shape of muck, or old
turfs from your hedge-rows, will add largely to your
compost heap, and in this way he will make up any
possible sacrifice in his flesh. Miss Martineau, I
know, in her 'Two Acre Farming,' advises severe
cleanliness; and if the only aim were a roaster for
your table and accumulation of fat, there might be
virtue in the recommendation. But a pig's work
among your turfs is worth half of his pork. He will
thrive very likely upon the waste from your table and
your garden. But, against any possible shortness of
food supply, it were well to provide a bag of what
the grain people will sell you as 'ship stuff;' and
this, stirred into the kitchen wash, will make an
unctuous holiday gruel for your little beast, for which
he will be clamorously grateful.

"Again; the stye should be convenient to the
garden (a hemlock spruce or two will shut off the
sight of it, and a sweet honey-suckle subdue the odors
of it); then you may throw over chance bits of purslane, or the suckers from your sweet corn, or a gone-
by salad, and find thanks in the noisy smacking of his
chops. I would not give a fig for a country house
where no such homely addenda are allowed, and
where a starched air of propriety must always reign,
to the complete exclusion of every stray weed, and to
the exclusion of the rollicking Suffolk grunter in its

corner, who squeals his entreaty, and declares thanks with the click-clack of his active jaws.

"He will take on larger and clumsier proportions month by month, and will be none the worse for the occasional carding which your zealous Irishman can afford him in spare hours; and when, in the month of October or November, the waste growth of the garden is abating, and the frost has nipped the bean-tops, and laid your tomatoes in a black sprawl upon the ground, your Suffolk (with, say, one or two additional bags of mixed feed) should be ripe for the knife.

"My advice, at this conjuncture, would be—sell him to the butcher. Those who like pig flesh better would give you rules for cut and curing. But, while I have considerable respect for the pork family when fairly afoot and showing grateful appreciation of the delights of life and of a full trough, I have very little consideration for the same animals when baked or stewed. Charles Lamb's pleasant eulogium on roast pig is one of the most terrible instigators of indigestion that I know; and I want no better theory for that charming writer's occasional periods of bitter despondency, than to suppose him to have dined 'at seven, sharp,' upon the dish he has so pleasantly and fearfully extolled.

"I do not mean to say that exception is not to be

made in favor of a good rasher of bacon at breakfast, with a fresh egg (from the cock—as a city friend once suggested in a flow of cheery, rural exuberance) ; nor do I think anything can be righteously said against a snug bit of clear pork in a dish of boiled corned brisket of beef; nay, I would still further extend the exception to a crisp fry of delicate slices as an accompaniment of grilled trout, where the latter fall below a half-pound in weight ; nor do I think great harm of a thin blanket of the same condiment to enwrap a roasted quail, or slivers of it to enlard delicately a fricandeau of veal. But, as for pork chops, or pork roast, or pork boiled, to be eaten as the chief piece nutritive of a dinner—it is an abomination ! Our friends the Jews have not only Scriptural reason in the thing, but reasons physiological.

"And now, my dear fellow, having despatched your pig (who should be bought for five or six dollars at seven weeks old, and should be sold at twenty— from the growth of your garden and a splicing bag of ship stuff), you will have, if you have used proper vigilance, some three to four loads of choice compost to contribute to the vegetable growth of the next season. There is a notion that manure from such a source provokes the growth of club-foot in cabbages and cauliflowers ; but after repeated trials with a view to fix this averment, I am unable to do so.

Club-foot is not lacking with awkward frequency; but appears quite as often, so far as my experience goes, with other fertilizers as with that from the pig stye. A good liming and fresh-turned soil are, so far as I can determine, the best preventives. Another precaution, which, in my view, should never be neglected, is to remove and destroy at once all plants which show symptoms of this ailment.

"The cow is a more tractable subject. Of course, you wish one that never kicks, that any one can milk, that will not resent indignities, and will yield you all the milk and the butter you need, and possibly the cheese.

"I remember that a city gentleman of great horticultural (and other) ability called upon me not many years ago, and after descanting upon the absurdity of planting two acres for a crop which could be easily grown from half an acre, he asked me how many quarts of milk my cows averaged per diem? 'Fourteen to fifteen quarts,' said I, 'in the flush season.'

"'But that is very small,' said he; 'there is no more reason why you should not have cows giving twenty to twenty-four quarts a day, than why you should not have strawberries giving two quarts to the plant.'

"I was not prepared to gainsay the proposition. The truth is, I feel a certain awe of distinguished

horticulturists that blinds me even to their wildest
assertions. What has an humble cultivator to do, or
to say, in the presence of a man who has bagged his
premiums at a New York Horticultural Society, and
is taster *ex-officio* at the Farmer's Club?

"I did not argue the matter with him; I submitted; I acknowledged my mediocrity humbly.

"Now, my dear fellow, there are cows which
yield their twenty to twenty-five quarts a day, but
they are very exceptional. Many such, whose private
history I have known, have been fed upon their own
milk with the cream taken off. This involves, as you
will admit, I think, a quick reconversion of capital,
which, with children in the family, is not always
practicable.

"In a general way, I should say, it would be far
safer to count upon an average of twelve to fifteen
quarts per day, even with the best of care. And as
regards your actual purchase of an animal, I dare say
you will have Wall Street friends, who will talk
grandly of the short horns, and suggest some Daisy,
(1397, A. H. B.,) at a cost of six or seven hundred
dollars, and—viewing her pedigree—cheap at that.
My advice to you is, don't buy any such, unless you
intend to turn breeder, and enter the lists with the
herd book people. I say this, not because the short-
horns are not admirable animals; but admirable ani-

mals are not always the best domestic animals,—as some of your recently married friends may possibly be able to testify.

"But a man who, like yourself, comes to the country for a leisurely enjoyment of all country bounties, does not wish an animal that must invariably be kept under the best possible condition; he wishes a docile, adaptable creature. Even a snug native beast might meet all the ends you would have in view, without figuring largely upon the cash book.

"Or, still better, a sleek Ayrshire, that shall carry in her air and horn a little show of better breeding and full returns to the milk pail. But if you have a fancy for cream that is fairly golden, and for occasional conversion of excess of milk into a little *pâté* of golden butter, nothing will suit your purpose better than a dainty Alderney, with her fawn-like eyes and yellow skin.

"I am aware that the short-horn people—who can see nothing good in a cow, except her figure show mathematical straightness of line from tail to the setting of her horn—sneer at the comparatively diminutive Alderneys. It is true, moreover, that there may be in them a hollow of the back, and an undue droop to the head, and possibly an angular projection of the hip-bones; but their nose is of the fineness of a fawn's, their eyes bright and quick as a doe's; their

skin soft and silken, and with a golden hue (if of
good family), which gives best of promise for the
cream-pot. Above all they have a tractability which,
in a domestic pet, is a most admirable quality. 'Spot,'
(the black and white Alderney,) the children can
fondle; she can be tethered to a stake upon the lawn,
and will feed as quietly as if she were in a field of
lucerne : she is grateful for a *bonne bouche* from the
garden, and takes it from the hand as kindly as a
dog. This docility is a thing of great consequence
upon a little country place where every animal is
made more or less of a pet. It is not every cow that
will bear tethering upon a lawn; there are those
indeed who can never be taught to submit to the
confinement. The sleek Alderneys inherit a capacity
for this thing, and I have seen upon the green
orchards near to St. Iiliers, (Isle of Jersey,) scores
of them, each cropping its little circlets of turf as
closely and cleanly as if it had been shorn. In way
of convenience for this service, it is well to have an
old harrow tooth with a ring adjusted to its top,
and revolving freely, upon which ring an iron swivel
should be attached. To such a fixture, easily moved,
and made fast in the ground by a blow or two of a
wooden mallet, a halter may be tied without fear of
any untwisting of the rope, or of any winding up or
other entrapment of the poor beast. I give these

hints because it is often convenient to furnish a pet cow, from time to time, some detached feeding ground, where the shrubbery will not admit of free rambling; and there are none whose habit is better adapted to such indulgence upon the lawn than the Alderneys.

"If your cow be kept up constantly for stall-feeding, an earthen floor is desirable, and by all means a half hour's run in the barn yard of a morning. A darkened shed will be a great luxury to her in fly time, and will largely promote the quiet under which she works out the most bountiful returns from the succulent food of the garden. A bit of ground in lucerne—say four rods square (it should be in drills and kept hoed the first season)—will yield an enormous amount of food material, and if convenient to the stall, your children will delight in binding it up in little sheaves for "Moolly." If such a bit of ground be so situated as to admit of an occasional sprinkling with liquid manure, five good cuts in a season may be safely counted on ; nor do I know any summer herbage which cows love better. Remember furthermore, that the lucerne, as well as corn fodder, is improved by a half day's wilting before being fed. In winter, the carrots and mangel wurtzel will become available ; both of which any cow may be taught to love, (if teaching be necessary,) by giving them a good sprinkling of meal. In the change from summer to winter diet, and from winter to summer, it must be remembered that all sudden changes from great succulence to dry food, or vice versa, is to be most cautiously avoided. Lack of care on this score, is the secret of half the cow ailments.

" If I were to lay down a pleasant and productive winter dietary for your Alderney, it would be a peck of sliced roots in the morning, not forgetting a lock of sweet hay; at noon, a quart or two of brewer's grains and fresh water *ad libitum ;* at night, a warm pailful of drink, into which a quart of coarsely ground buckwheat meal shall have been stirred, and another lock of sweet hay in way of nightcap.

" With such food, and an occasional combing, at the hands of Patrick, (all the better if daily,) I think you may count upon such golden returns of cream as will bring back a taste of the grassy spring-time."

Thus much for Lackland's Pig and Cow.

On Gateways.

I HAVE often wondered why the professional writers on landscape gardening have so little to say of gateways. Among the more pretentious authors of this class I find sketches of gate-lodges, very charming in their details, many of them ; but I find little or no mention of those modest gates which

4

must hang at every man's door-yard—those unpretending swinging barriers, by which every country house-holder is shut off from the world, and by which he is joined to the world. They may be made to give a good deal of expression to a place; they have almost as much to do with it, in fact, as a man's mouth has to do with the expression of his face.

There was once a gate called " Beautiful," by which a lame man lay—we all remember that; there was once too a certain " wicket-gate " (with a great light shining somewhere beyond it) which Evangelist pointed out to Christian, whereby the pilgrim might enter upon the path to the Celestial City—we all remember that gate; and there was another gate, belonging to our days of roundabouts and satchels, by which we went out, noon and morning, by which we returned, noon and evening—on which we swung upon stolen occasions—a gate whereat we loitered with other philosophers, in other roundabouts and with other green satchels, and discussed problems of marbles, or base-ball, or of the weather,—a gate through which led the path to the first home; well, I think everybody remembers such a gate. And thus it happens that the subject has a certain poetic and romantic interest which cannot be wholly ignored, and which I wonder that the landscapists have so indifferently treated.

Fancy, if you can, a rural home,—without its gate-way—lying all abroad upon a common! The great charm of privacy is gone utterly; and no device of shrubbery, or hedge, can make good the loss of some little wicket which will invite approach, and be a barrier against too easy familiarity. The creak of the gate-hinge is a welcome to the visitor, and as he goes out, the latch clicks an adieu.

But there are all sorts of gates, as there are all sorts of welcomes; there is, first, your inhospitable one, made mostly, I should say, of matched boards, with a row of pleasant iron spikes running along its top, and no architectural decorations of pilaster or panel can possibly remove its thoroughly inhospitable aspect. It belongs to stable-courts or jail-yards, but never to a home or to a garden.

Again, there are your ceremonious gates, of open-work indeed, but ponderous, and most times scrupulously closed; the very opening of them is a fatiguing ceremonial, and there is nothing like a lively welcome in the dull clang of their ponderous latches.

Next, there is your simple, unpretending, rural gate, giving promise of unpretending rural beauties—homely in all its aspect, and giving foretaste of the best of homeliness within. And I make a wide distinction here between the simple rurality at which I have hinted, and that grotesqueness which is com-

passed by scores of crooked limbs and knots wrought
into labyrinthine patterns, which puzzle the eye, more

than they please. All crooked things are not necessarily charming, and the better kind of homeliness is
measured by something besides mere roughness.

Lastly, there is your hospitable gate, with its little
rooflet stretched over it, as if to invite the stranger
loiterer to partake at his will of that much of the
hospitalities of the home. Even the passing beggar
gathers his tattered garments under it in a sudden
shower and blesses the shelter. And I introduce upon
the next page a very homely specimen of this class of
gates, which I remember to have sketched many
years ago somewhere in County Kent, England.

Either my own pencillings were very bad, or else
the engraver has failed to give the character of its
rough rooflet ; which, if I remember rightly, was but

a thatch of broom, or of sedge. Yet who does not see written all over it—plain as it is : Loiter if you like ! Come in, if you like ! And I love to think that

some little maid, under it—in some by-gone year—said her good-night to some parting Leander. Who shall laugh at this, that has ever been young ? Are not the little maids and the Leanders always growing up about us ? I always felt sure when I found such covered wickets that no curmudgeon lived within.

A second example of somewhat more orderly proportions, but identical in expression, I take from my note-book of travel, finding it credited to some little hamlet of Warwickshire ; the posts and supporting arms being of unhewn elm, and the roof a neat thatch of wheat straw, which at the time of my visit was gray and mossy.

Has not somebody somewhere a cottage home, whose homeliness would be enforced and beautified by such a cosy covered wicket of thatch ?

Thatch, indeed, does not take on with us, and

under our climate, that mellow mossiness which belongs to it in Devonshire. Our winds are too high
and drying, and the sun too hot. Still, a thatch properly laid will, with us, keep its evenness for a great
number of years ; and for the benefit of those living
within easy reach of the coast, I may say that nothing
is better for this purpose than the sedge (so called)
of the salt marshes.

In default of thatch, however, very pretty rural
effects may be made by slabs (being log-trimmings
from the saw-mills), or oak bark (which is almost
imperishable), or by scolloped shingles.

An example of the effect of these latter I venture
to give.

In this case, all beneath the roof is of cedar with
the bark undisturbed, while the posts above the roof
are trimmed to a square, tapering and carrying a ball
—the balls and the tapering extremities of the posts

being painted white, and the roof red. The effect is exceedingly good—though it mixes the rustic and

more finished work in a way which the professional artists do not venture upon. But I have lived long enough to know that professional traditions in all the arts—landscape gardening and architecture among the rest—stand in the way of a great many beauties. Every country-place wants its special art-garniture (without respect to traditions) as much as every pretty face wants its special environment of colors and of laces. When, therefore, I hear a man declaim against white gates, or red gates, or rustic gates, or stone gates, *per se*, without reference to their position,

or suggestive aims, I condemn him as an iron method-
ist, who apprehends no beauty by intuition, but only
by force of precept.

Perhaps I have myself rather hastily condemned
all close gates, as belonging to stable-courts and jail-
yards. There are situations, certainly, where they
are not only allowable, (as upon back-entrances of
gardens,) but where they contribute eminently to the
air of privacy which must mark every true home.
And I am reminded, in this connection, of a certain
garden-door-way, which I saw near Keightley, in
Yorkshire; it opened upon a narrow lane in the rear

of the suburban grounds to which it was attached,
and showed such homely, resolute determination to
work up into tasteful shape the stones abounding in
the neighborhood, that I made a rough draught of it
upon the spot.

This picturesque use of rock material is appreciated and practised in many parts of Great Britain.
Thus in the neighborhood of the slate quarries of

North Wales, near Caernarvon, the refuse material from the ledges is laid up by the adjoining proprietors in snug fences, that appear at a little distance away, to be crowned with a regularly castellated battlement. This effect is produced simply by alternating cubical and oblong fragments of slate rock upon the summit of the wall.

In Derbyshire, again, I have seen a kindred effect wrought by the tasteful disposition of the big boulders which are scattered pretty thickly over some of the high moorlands of that country. In Cumberland and Westmoreland, indications of the same rural adaptiveness abound.

Thus much has been suggested at present by our friend Lackland's request that I should supply for him the plan of a gate. We will now see what can be done for his special needs.

Gateways and Rural Carpentry.

ON turning back to page of ground plan, the reader will perceive, from the drawing of my friend Lackland's grounds, that he has need of three principal gateways—a small one for the footpath, being the entrance nearest to the village ; a larger one for his drive, and a third opening for his grass field. This last he will not have very frequent occa-

4*

sion to use; for that reason the gateway should not be very striking, or seem specially to invite entrance. Supposing that the occupant has availed himself of the old walls about the premises to build a substantial stone fence along a considerable portion of his front, I should advise that he mark this field entrance by two substantial columns built of the same material, and place between them a gate or movable panel of fence, constructed of cedar poles, or such other homely or lasting wood as may be most available.

I give a rough drawing of what I would propose.

I think that everyone will admit that these columns have a tasteful effect, and add largely to the architectural character of the wall. And it is a great mistake to suppose, as many do, that such columns require hammered stone, or that it is requisite that they be laid up in mortar, and by an adept in masonry. All that is required is, that stones carrying fairly developed angles should be laid aside for its construction—that the face of the column should project three or four inches from the surface of the wall in order to mark distinctly its faces, and that it be bound in firmly, (a thing which the engraver has omitted to do,) with such long stones as are available. A boulder sufficiently round to crown the structure may be found in almost any rod of old country wall; and if it be well covered with lichens, so much the better. The great error in such attempts, is in attempting too great nicety, which, by contrast with the homely farmwork around it, offends more than it gratifies. In humble art, as well as in the highest art, there must be keeping.

But though finical nicety is to be avoided, and such hammering out of faces, as to increase largely the expense, and defeat the economy which should declare itself unmistakably in all rural decoration, there should be no sacrifice of solidity. A column that will not stand for years, had better never be built.

The country wall-layers, ordinarily, are indisposed to attempt such work, either doubting their own capacity, or considering it an encroachment upon the province of the mason. The consequence has been, in my own experience, that of some half-dozen or more which stand here and there about the fields at Edgewood, every one has been laid up with my own hands; and I may aver, with some pride, that after eight or ten winters of frost, they still stand firmly and compact. One only has lost its capping boulder, which certain errant boys could not resist the temptation to tumble off, that they might watch its roll down a pretty declivity of a hundred rods, or more. I wish I had no more grievous charges to bring against errant boys.

For the entrance to the drive-way, supposing that my friend Lackland has plenty of cedar at hand, I give another design :

And I have this much to say in favor of it, that a similar one was erected at Edgewood eleven years since, and its gates have swung back and forth a dozen times a day, without, as yet, a single hammer's stroke in way of repair.

The dotted lines upon the right half of the gate

indicate two half-inch iron rods, which were passed through and fastened by a nut upon the longer upright sapling. Once or twice it has been necessary to give this nut a turn or two with the wrench, and this completes the tale of the attention it has required.

The first panel (and part of the second) of the fence to which it is attached, is given to show its relation to its surroundings, and the perfect simplicity of detail which belongs to it. The posts are firm and cannot swag. The gates are light—perfectly braced, and held in place by the iron rods which pass through them. They bid fair to last until the sap portion of the wood (cedar) is fairly rotted away. The three horizontal arms are inserted with tenons; the braces are fitted only with the gouge, and made fast with wire nails. And here I wish to enter a plea for the wire nails, used all over the continent of Europe, but, as yet, little known with us; though, I believe, they are to be found in the larger hardware shops of New York. The advantage of them is, that they can be driven without splitting the wood—that they can be clenched effectively, and—what is of importance in light work—they add very little to the weight. For the construction of interior rustic work of twigs and bark they are invaluable. They may be found of all sizes, from that of a cambric needle (and a half-inch in length) to that corresponding to our " ten pennies," and lighter by two-thirds than these.

The third gate is equally simple, and in way of ornamentation, has only its little rooflet. The design represents this as of equal width with the gate; but a somewhat better effect may be secured by an extension of the roof some six or eight inches on either side, in which case, of course, the posts must be cut off even with the ridge, and finials of cedar sticks adjusted at either end. This bit of roof over the gateway gives not only the hospitable air, which I remarked upon in the previous chapter, but serves to protect the rustic work from the weather to such a degree that the bark will hold fast for double the length of time. In all such work, great annoyance is given by an insect which devours the sapwood under the bark, thus loosening the latter, and filling it with an ugly yellow powder. I have observed, in my own experience, that the ravages of this insect are much more decided and constant upon cedar cut in the winter, than upon such as has been cut in the growing season of the year. The fact, however, may be accidental, and I must confess utter ignorance of the habits and tastes of this disagreeable grub.

The virtue of all such rustic work as I have commented upon, lies in its exceeding simplicity, joined to great serviceableness. Home repairs do not tell badly on it; the joints need not be arranged with mathematical precision; the materials are near at hand and inexpensive; the creeping vines cling to it lovingly; it wears age with a veteran sturdiness.

I am by no means prepared to say that my friend Lackland will adopt my views on this head. I suspect that his country or city joiner, when confronted with the hints I have thrown out in these gate sketches, (they are really intended for nothing more than hints), will shake his head doubtfully, and lay before my friend some stupendous affair of carpentry, with an infinitude of mouldings, which, to his eye, is vastly finer. And I shall expect Lackland to yield to the charm of the rectangular elevations that are set before him; or, if he absolutely insists upon the working up of what stray cedars, or other wood, may be about the premises, I shall expect his carpenter to make such a bugbear of the exuding pitch, and of the impossibility of bringing his square and his gauge into requisition, and (if he goes on) to keep so resolutely by a determination to counterfeit, as far as possible, all the mouldings of his joiner work, that he will construct a cumbrous affair, at such great cost of labor, as will disgust my friend Lackland, and at such cost of simplicity as will disgust every tasteful observer.

What then? There can be no doubt of the possibility of working this unruly material into tasteful forms, that shall have practical and economic uses ; but in the ordering of this matter, as in the ordering of a great many others, connected with rural life, if the proprietor can put no zeal into his intention, and has no eye for the charms of homeliness, let him abandon the pursuit. A good fence of white pickets, with gate to match, will keep the pigs out, and the young Lacklands in.

Village and Country Road-side.

EVERY Christian dweller, in village or in country, owes a duty to his road-side ; which, if he neglects, he relapses—horticulturally speaking—into heathenism. This duty is to maintain order and neat-

ness; and he is no more relieved of this duty because
the highway is assigned over to public uses, than
he is relieved of any other duty whose accomplishment must of necessity contribute to the public
convenience and public education, as well as to his
own. Because my front entry is shared, for all legitimate purposes, with my friends and chance callers,
shall I therefore treat it with neglect and allow the
dust and cobwebs to accumulate about it, while I
ensconce myself churlishly in my well-swept den?
Yet, every visitor—unless he be a vagabond fruit-
stealer, or an equally vagabond bird-killer—comes up
the road-way, and if you choose to put him through a
course of scoriæ, and old tins, and tansy tufts, and
briary heaps of stones along your road-side, you
might as benevolently and as prudently, (so far as the
growing tastes of your children are concerned,) lead
him up to your front door between piles of gaping
clam shells. There is no rule of order, or of taste, or
of benevolence, that belongs to a man's door-yard,
that does not belong to his road-side.

It is true, there is a liability outside the fence to
the incursions of road-menders, who are, for the most
part, barbarians; but there is no more reason for not
covering or removing the odious traces of these animals, than for not removing the disagreeable traces
of others. An ugly yellow scar in the turfy mound

that supports, maybe, your garden wall, by due attention, and a shovel full or two of fresh mould, can be thoroughly obliterated; but if submitted to the swash of the rains, it gapes and throws off a great ooze of yellow mud, which, next spring time, tempts the foraging shovel of the road-menders again, and in a few years your whole road-side is a disorderly line of jagged earth-pits, with raw boulders clustering at the front of each. A little timely care, often repeated, may at last win upon the regard of the barbarian followers of the scraper and hoe, and they may grow unwittingly into a respect for your love of order Such miracles are subject of record. A safer alternative, however, if your road-side be no more extensive than that of my friend Lackland, is to supply, at your own cost, an occasional defect in the road-bed from the screenings of the coal, or the rakings of the garden, by which you may easily secure so even and compact a surface, as to escape the attention of the road viewers. If, on the other hand, the reach be long, an arrangement can sometimes be made with the select-men to keep its whole extent in perfect condition, for a sum which, if it be small, will be remunerative in the exemption it gives.

I say sometimes such convention may be established by an order-loving individual, but not always. Your true old-style representative of a select-man always scents some party bargain, or sly scheme in such a proposition—most of all if the proposals run below current rates. Indeed, if it were desirable for prudential reasons to keep the world from revolving as it does, I think the matter (if feasible) could be most safely entrusted to the " select-men " of a country town. I do not know any better types of old fogyism than the average of black-coated select-men, who will meet ten evenings to discuss a nine-penny bridge, and spend six months of consideration upon the opening of six rods of new highway. If the Pacific Railway is ever completed, (as I hope it may be,) I would suggest that a committee of " select-men " from our country towns (with a change of linen and the last week's paper) be put through on the first car,—in the hope of opening their eyes to at least one current fact of the age. I am sometimes tortured with the notion that after twenty years of spectacled observation, (I do not yet wear spectacles,) and after twenty years of voting the " rig'lar " ticket, I may become a candidate for the office of select-man. The thought oppresses me like a night-mare.

To return to road-side,—I know nothing which contributes more to that air of thrift, which should belong to every country township, than neat and orderly road-sides ; and when I say neat and orderly, I do not mean any finical arrangement of turf, or clip-

ping of the road-track, but only such judicious combing down of unsightly roughnesses, such watchfulness against encumbrance, such adaptation of existing shade trees, or such planting of others, as shall
show that the adjoining proprietor does not limit his
charities by his own walls, or his eye for neatness by
the line of highway.

Once upon a time, when the writer was in search of
a country homestead, he remembers deciding against
certain " strongly recommended " places, because the
highroad to them led through a considerable array of suburban houses, whose occupants made it a
religious duty to throw all their offal in the public
street, and to cumber the same locality with their
hoop-poles, or their wood-piles, or their shoe-parings.
It is so hard to unlearn such a noisome depravity of
taste! Many of the small towns on the banks of the
Hudson (near to New York) and in New Jersey,
offer an extended exhibition of this sort of local economy and fragrant treasures. And I have sometimes
thought that New York citizens, by reason of the
offal in their streets, become quite agreeably wonted
to such disposition of cast-away bones and filth, and
scent it, upon their drives to their country homes,
with an appetizing relish. But in the name of all
true rural delight, I beg to enter protest, and to urge
every man who has his homestead under green trees,

to use what influence may lie in him (albeit he is not select-man) to abate the nuisance, and to make our village and country road-sides smack of order and thrift and cleanliness. Good example will do very much in way of reform—more, in most instances, than any zeal of preachment. If you approach an old-school neighbor, who has inherited the propensity to cumber the highway before his door with all conceivable odds and ends, with any suggestions for a change on the score of neatness or good looks, you will find him, very likely, fortified with his own " idees " on that subject—" idees," which, like the independent American citizen that he is, he is in no mood to relinquish.

" He can't git a livin by looks," and with such speech shrewdly uttered, and emphasized with a rattling horse-laugh, he floors your blandest suggestions. Yet a wholesome attention to neatness on your own score, which shall creep up to the edge of his enclosures, and work by contrast, will in time operate insensibly upon him.—There is something after all " very catching " in good order.

But most of all, the co-operation of all the town's people, who are disposed to neatness, is to be relied upon. Every country place of any size should have its " village-improvement society," to look after the planting of shade trees, the proper condition of highways, the arrest of stray cattle, and to discuss and carry into execution whatever may promote the thrift and attractive appearance of the place,—whether in the way of new streets, laying down of side-walks, or removal of offensive debris or noxious weeds. I commend most heartily to Lackland the instigation and establishment of such a society. And if such a club could have their little room for occasional meeting, and stock it with a few valuable horticultural and agricultural books and papers, so much the better. An entirely new air might be given to very many of our slatternly country villages in a few years, by the energetic operations of such a club, and the value and attractiveness of property be correspondingly increased.

Most of the North-eastern States have, within a few years, by legislative enactment, outlawed all strolling cattle. This is well, and relieves from a great nuisance. But in not a few broad-streeted towns there has sprung up in consequence, a rank growth of weeds, (formerly kept down by grazing cows,) which, as it seems no individual's concern, are allowed to ripen their seeds, thus multiplying next year's labor in the fields, besides offering a terribly straggling appearance. In fault of such co-operative club as I have hinted at, (which should order them cut at common expense,) every man should see to his own frontage. If such nursery beds had not been tolerated, we should long ago, I think, have scotched the Canada thistle, if not that detestable weed, the wild carrot.

At a considerable remove from towns, we frequently come upon some quiet streak of country road, charmingly bordered with a wild sylvan tangle of hickories, sumacs, brambles, cedars, and all festooned perhaps with the tendrils of the wild grape, or the bittersweet. Neither economy or good taste command the removal of these, even when bordering cultivated fields, except (which rarely occurs) they harbor bad weeds to spread within the enclosure. Nay, in nine cases in ten they furnish a grateful shelter from the winds,—a matter too little appreciated as yet, either by fruit growers or grain growers. And on the score of taste, no more charming contrast can be devised than that of such wild profusion of growth, with the neat and orderly array of crops beyond. I can recall no more delightful rural scenes in England, than certain ones in Devonshire, where, after strolling along some admirable bit of Macadam, with high hedge-rows on either side, sprinkled with primroses, and tasselled with nodding ferns, and wild with tangled thickets of bramble, I have, with a leap, broken through and seen beyond,—so near the road I could have tossed my hat into the field,—such trim lines of emerald wheat,—without ever a weed or a crook, —as made the heart rejoice. The high hedge-rows are indeed now being cut down throughout the best cultivated districts, but only for the economy of land, the surface occupied being needed. But while we have country roads from five to six rods wide, the same objection does not obtain with us. Observe again, I beg, that I do not counsel the planting of any such road-side tangles, or indeed the sparing of them, when *any better use can be made of the land.* I only plead for their continued presence in place of a rude hurly-burly of stubs and harsh boulders, to which condition many farmers reduce them, and call it a judicious " slicking up."

I have run widely away from the little homestead of my friend Lackland; so widely indeed, that I shall not soon encounter him again. Whenever that may be, I trust I may hear that his pelargoniums are all a-bloom—that his pig and his cow are thriving—his road-side in order,—his Patrick a jewel of a man, and that all rural felicities attend him.

WAY-SIDE HINTS.

5

III.

WAY-SIDE HINTS.

Talk about Porches.

A COUNTRY house without a porch is like a man without an eyebrow; it gives expression, and gives expression where you most want it. The least office of a porch is that of affording protection against the rain-beat and the sun-beat. It is an interpreter of character; it humanizes bald walls and windows; it emphasizes architectural tone; it gives hint of hospitality; it is a hand stretched out (figuratively and lumberingly, often) from the world within to the world without.

At a church door even, a porch seems to me to be a blessed thing, and a most worthy and patent demonstration of the overflowing Christian charity, and of the wish to give shelter. Of all the images of wayside country churches which keep in my mind, those hang most persistently and agreeably, which show their jutting, defensive rooflets to keep the brunt of the storm from the church-goer while he yet fingers at the latch of entrance.

I doubt if there be not something beguiling in a porch over the door of a country shop—something that relieves the odium of bargaining, and imbues even the small grocer with a flavor of cheap hospitalities. The verandas (which is but a long translation of porch) that stretch along the great river front of the Bellevue Hospital, diffuse somehow a gladsome cheer over that prodigious caravansery of the sick; and I never see the poor creatures in their bandaged heads and their flannel gowns enjoying their convalescence in the sunshine of those exterior corridors, but I reckon the old corridors for as much as the young doctors, in bringing them from convalescence into strength, and a new fight with the bedevilments of the world.

What shall we say, too, of inn porches? Does anybody doubt their fitness? Is there any question of the fact—with any person of reasonably imaginative mood—that Falstaff and Nym and Bardolph, and the rest, once lolled upon the benches of the porch that overhung the door of the Boar's Head Tavern, Eastcheap? Any question about a porch, and a generous one, at the Taberd, Southwark—presided over by that wonderful host who so quickened the story-telling humors of the Canterbury pilgrims of Master Chaucer ?

Then again, in our time, if one were to peel away the verandas and the exterior corridors from our vast watering-place hostelries, what an arid baldness of wall and of character would be left ! All sentiment, all glowing memories, all the music of girlish foot-falls, all echoes of laughter and banter and rollicking mirth, and tenderly uttered vows would be gone.

King David, when he gave out to his son Solomon the designs for the building of the Temple, included among the very first of them (1 Chron. xxviii. 11) the "pattern of a porch." It is not, however, of porches of shittim-wood and of gold that I mean to talk just now—nor even of those elaborate architectural features which will belong of necessity to the entrance-way of every complete study of a country house. I plead only for some little mantling hood about every exterior door-way, however humble.

There are hundreds of naked, vulgar-looking dwellings, scattered up and down our country high-roads, which only need a little deft and adroit adaptation of the hospitable feature which I have made the subject of this paper, to assume an air of modest grace, in place of the present indecorous exposure of a wanton.

But let no one suppose that porch-building, as
applied to the homely lines of a staid old house of
thirty or fifty years since, can be safely given over to
the judgment of our present ambitious carpenters.
Ten to one, they will equip a barren simplicity with
an odious tawdriness. A town-bred girl will slip
into the millinery bedizenment of the town haber-
dasher without making show of any odious incon-
gruity ; but let some buxom, round-cheeked, stout-
ankled lass of the back country adopt the same, and
we laugh at the enormity. In the same way, every
man of a discerning taste must smile derisively at the
adornment of an unpretentious farm-house with the
startling decorative features of the shop joinery of
the day—the endless scroll-work (done cheaply, by
new methods of machine sawing)—the portentous
moulding—the arches, whose outlines are from By-
zantium or the new Louvre—columns whose proportions are improved from the Greeks—capitals whose
fretting sculpture outranks the acanthus. Seriously,
I think the carpenters, if left to their own efflo-
rescence, now-a-days, can out-match Demorest or any
of the wide-hooped milliners. We seem to have
drifted into an epoch of the largest and crudest flam-
boyance—in morals, in brokerage, in carpentry, in
(may I not say ?) congressional eloquence. A sober,
simple-minded man is worse than lost in the new
brood of improvers.

Notwithstanding all this, I venture to plead for a wholesome severity of taste; if simple material is to be dealt with, it should be dealt with simply. If we have a homely old-style house to modify and render attractive, do not let us make its modification a mockery by the blazon of Chinese scroll-work. There is a way of dealing with what is old, in keeping with what is old, and of dealing with what is homely, in keeping with what is homely. A sensible middle-aged lady of the old school, if she have occasion to present herself afresh in society, and assert her prerogatives once more, will not surely do so by tying tow-bags at the back of her head and widening her skirts indecorously. But she will bring her old manner with her, and so equip the old manner by the devices of a judicious art that we shall wonder and admire in spite of ourselves.

In illustration of my views about homely porches, I venture to give upon the next page a rough drawing of one of the plainest conceivable. It is a sort of cross between the Dutch stoop and the lumbering rooflet which in old times overhung many a doorway of a New England farm-house. It offers shelter and rest; it is in no way pretentious; it declares its character at a glance; you cannot laugh at it for any air of assumption that it carries; you can find no such shapen thing in any of the architectural books,

What then? Must it needs be condemned for this reason?

I do not, indeed, commend it for any beauty, *per se*, but as being an honest, well-intended shelter and resting-place, which could be grafted upon many an

old-style farm-house, with bare door, and set off its barrenness, with quaint, simple lines of hospitality, that would add more to the real effect of the home than a cumbrous series of joiner's arches of tenfold its cost. In the door itself I have dropped a hint of many an ancient door which confronts the high-road in a score of New England villages. People do not instruct their carpenters to build such doors now; yet I can conceive of worse ones, glazed up and down, with blue and yellow and green glass, in most irritating conjunction. I do not know that I would absolutely advise the building of those ancient divided doors with their diamond " lights ; " but wherever they show their quaint faces, looking out tranquilly upon the clash and turmoil of our latter half of the century, I would certainly cherish them ; or if I hung a porch over them, it would be such a one as should be in keeping with their quaintness, and yet offer all promise—which a sensible porch should offer—of shelter and rest. There is a village I never pass through but I ache to clap over one or more of its old-time doors (now battling without vestige of roof-let, with sun and rain) some such quaint, overhang-ing beacon of hospitality as I have pictured ; I am sure the houses would take on a double homeliness, and I should think of all the inmates as growing thenceforth, every day, more kindly, and every day mellower in their charities.

I next give a sketch of a little stone porch, which, if I do not mistake, is taken from some stone cottage in Cumberland County, England. It belongs, certain-ly, by its whole air and by its arrangement, to a country where stones of good, straight-splitting qual-ity (such as gneiss) are plentiful, and are used for unpretending cottage architecture. It would seem to have pertained to a house of very modest character

5*

and to one whose position and exposure demanded
special shelter. I think it may offer a hint, at least,
of the proper use of similar material in our country.
We have not half learned yet all that may be accomplished in domestic architecture, with the wealth of
stones scattered over our fields. Dear lumber is
teaching us somewhat; but necessity will presently
teach us more. The great cost of mason-work is in
the way of any present large use of stone for building
purposes, least of all such purpose as a cottage porch.
But with straight-cleaving stone at hand, such a
porch as I have drawn could be put together, with
all its real effect (though not perhaps a great nicety),
by common wall-layers; and it is for this reason I
have introduced it, hoping that some intelligent pro-

prietor who is in the neighborhood of quarries will
put his hands to the task of imitation.

I give still another design copied rudely from
an actual porch at Ambleside (Westmoreland); it
was shading the door, some fifteen years since, of

a village curate. There were vines clambering over
it, which I have omitted, in order to give a full idea
of the simplicity of its construction. I know it is the
way of the grand architects to sneer at all rustic
work as child's play; but I cannot see the pertinence
of their sneers; it is quite true that rustic work will
not last forever—neither will we; house-holders and
architects, and all the rest of us, have the worms
gnawing at our vitals, and the bark falling away, and

the end coming swift. But a good, stanch tree trunk,
cut in its best season (late autumn), is a very toler-
able sort of God's work, and, seems to me, can be put
to very picturesque uses. I don't think the curate's
porch is a bad one ; as a hint for better ones, I think
it is specially good.

Upon the question of the use of right material for
rustic work, there is very much to be said ; here, I
have only space for a suggestion or two. There are
some trees which hold their bark wonderfully well ;
of such is the sassafras, which, after its tenth year,
takes on a picturesque roughness and a rhinoceros-
like thickness of skin, which admirably fits it for
rustic use. The white ash, assuming after fifteen
years a similar thickness of outer covering, holds its
coat with almost equal tenacity. The ordinary "pig-
nut" hickory holds its bark well ; the oak does not ;
neither does the chestnut. The cedar is perhaps most
commonly employed for rustic decoration ; cut in the
proper season, and due precaution being taken, by
coating of oil or varnish, against the ravages of the
grubs (which have an uncommon appetite for the
sapwood of cedar), it may hold its shaggy epidermis
for a long time. I would suggest to those using it
for architectural purposes a wash of crude petroleum ;
it is a wash that, so far as I know, is proof against
the appetite of all insects. Its objectionable odor

soon passes away. Very many of the smooth-barked trees, such as beech, birch, maple, and sycamore, will hold their bark firmly if precautions be taken to exclude the air by varnishing the ends and all such cuts as have been made by the excision of a limb. Old and slow-growing wood will, it must be observed, have less shrinkage, and maintain a better bark surface, than young saplings or trees of rapid growth. But, irrespective of all questions of durability, is there not something rurally attractive in this unpretending porch, whose columns have come from the forest, and whose overarching arms are the arms that overarch God's temples of the wood? Not lacking, surely, some elements of the beautiful in itself; and at the door of a village clergyman, with the ivy showing its glossy leaflets in wealthy labyrinth, and the convolvulus twining up at the base upon whatever vine-hold may offer, and handing out its purple chalices to catch the dews of the morning—is there nothing to be emulated in this? Let those who love God's simplest graces, answer.

On Not Doing All at Once.

THERE are a great many ardently progressive people who will be shocked by the caption under which I write. The current American theory is, that if a thing needs to be done, it should be done at once,—with railroad speed, no matter whether it regards politics, morals, religion, or horticulture. And I wantonly take the risk of being condemned for an arrant conservative, when I express my belief that there are a great many good objects in life which are accomplished better by gradual progression toward them than by sudden seizure. I shall not stay to argue the point with respect to negro suffrage, or female suffrage, or a temperance reformation, or the clearing out of Maximilian's Mexican Imperialism—which are a little removed from the horticultural arena, where our humbler questions are discussed—but I shall urge a graduation and culmination of triumphs in what relates to rural life and its charms.

One meets, from time to time, with a gentleman from the city, smitten with a sudden rural fancy, who is in eager search for a place "made to his hand," with the walks all laid down, the entrance-ways established, the dwarf trees regularly planted, the conservatory a-steam, and the crocheted turrets fretting the sky-line of the suburban villa. But I never heard of any such seeker after perfected beauties who was an enthusiast in country pursuits, or who did not speedily grow weary of his phantasy. He may take a pride in his cheap bargain ; he may regale himself with the fruits and enjoy the vistas of his arbor ; but he has none of that exquisitely-wrought satisfaction which belongs to the man who has planted his own trees, who has laid down his own walks, and who has seen, year after year, successive features of beauty in shrub, or flower, or pathway, mature under his ministering hand, and lend their attractions to the cumulating charms of his home. The man of capital, who buys into an established business, where the system is perfected, the trade regular and constant, the details unvaried, may very possibly congratulate himself upon the security of his gains; but he knows nothing of that ardent and intoxicating enthralment which belongs to one who has grown up with the business—suggested its enterprises—shared its anxieties, and by thought, and struggle, and adventure, made himself a part of its successes.

A man may enjoy a little complacency in wearing the coat of another, (if he gets it cheap,) but there can hardly be much pride in it. Therefore, I would say to any one who is thoroughly in earnest about a country home—make it for yourself. Xenophon, who lived in a time when Greeks were Greeks, advised people in search of a country place to buy of a slatternly and careless farmer, since in that event they might be sure of seeing the worst, and of making their labor and care work the lar-

gest results. Cato,* on the other hand, who represented a more effeminate and scheming race,
advised the purchase of a country home from a
good farmer and judicious house-builder, so that the
buyer might be sure of nice culture and equipments,
—possibly at a bargain. It illustrates, I think, rather
finely, an essential difference between the two races
and ages :—the Greek, earnest to make his own brain
tell, and the Latin, eager to make as much as he could
out of the brains of other people.

I must say that I like the Greek view best. I
never knew of an enthusiast in any pursuit,—whether
grape-growing, or literature, or ballooning, or politics,—who did not find his chiefest pleasure in fore-
casting successes, not yet made, but only dimly conceived of, and ardently struggled for. The more
enthusiasm, the more evidence, I should say, in a
general way, of incompletion and apparent confusion.

Show me a cultivator whose vines are well
trained by plumb and line, whose trees are every one
planted mathematically in quincunx order, whose
dwarfs are all clipped and braced after the best pyramidal pattern, and I feel somehow that he is a fash-
ionist, that he reposes upon certain formulas beyond

* I shall make no apology for the introduction of these two
heathen names, since both authors have written capitally well on
subjects connected with husbandry and rural life.

which he does not think it necessary to explore. But
where I see, with an equal degree of attention, irreg-
ularity and variety of treatment,—tendrils a-droop
and fruit-spurs apparently neglected,—I am not unfrequently impressed with the belief that the cultivator is regardless of old and patent truths, because
their truth is proven, and because his eye and mind
are on the strain toward some new development.

When a good, kind horticultural gentleman takes
me by the button-hole, and tells me by the hour of
what length it is necessary to cut the new wood in
order to insure a good start for the buds at the base,
and how the sap has a tendency to flow strongest into
the taller shoots, and other such truisms, which have
been in the books these ten years, I listen respectfully, but cannot help thinking,—" my dear good sir,
you will never set the river a-fire."

Nor indeed do we want the river set on fire; but
we want progress. And all I have said thus far is
but preliminary to the truth on which I wish to insist,
—that a graduated progress is essential to all rational
enjoyment, whether in things rural, Christian, or commercial.

And for this reason I allege that all things which
are proper to be done about a country house, are not
to be done at once. Half the charm of life in such a
home is in every week's and every season's succeed-

ing developments. If, for instance, my friend Lackland, whose place I have described in previous pages,
had found a landscape gardener capable of inaugurat-
ing all the changes I have described, and had established his garden, his mall, his shrubberies, and had
made the cliff in the corner nod with its blooming
columbines, within a month after occupation, and
established his dwarf pears in full growth and fruitage, there may have been a glad surprise; but the
very completeness of the change would have left no
room for that exhilaration of spirits, with which we
pursue favorite aims to their attainment. No trout-
fisher, who is worthy the name, wants his creel
loaded in the beginning; he wants the pursuit—the
alternations of hope and fear; the coy rest of his fly
upon this pool—the whisk of its brown hackle down
yonder rapid—its play upon the eddies where possibly some swift strike may be made—the sway of his
rod, and the whiz of his reel under the dash of some
struggling victim.

It is a mistake, therefore, I think, to aim at the
completion of a country home in a season, or in two,
or some half a dozen. Its attractiveness lies, or
should lie, in its prospective growth of charms. Your
city home—when once the architect, and plumber,
and upholsterer have done their work—is in a sense
complete, and the added charms must lie in the genial

socialities and hospitalities with which you can invest it ; but with a country home, the fields, the flowers, the paths, the hundred rural embellishments, may be made to develop a constantly recurring succession of attractive features. This year, a new thicket of shrubbery, or a new gate-way on some foot-path ; next year, the investment of some out-lying ledge with floral wonders ; the season after may come the establishment of a meadow (by judicious drainage) where some ugly marsh has offended the eye ; and the succeeding summer may show the redemption of the harsh briary up-land that you have scourged into fertility and greenness. This year, a thatched rooflet to some out-lying stile ; next year, a rustic seat under the trees which have begun to offer a tempting shade. This year, the curbing of the limbs of some over-growing poplar ; and next year—if need be—a lopping away of the tree itself to expose a fresher beauty in the shrubbery beneath.

Most planters about a country home are too much afraid of the axe ; yet judicious cutting is of as much importance as planting ; and I have seen charming thickets shoot up into raw, lank assemblage of boles of trees without grace or comeliness, for lack of courage to cut trees at the root. For all good effects of foliage in landscape gardening—after the fifth year— the axe is quite as important an implement as the spade. Even young trees of eight or ten years growth which stool freely—(such as the soft maple, birch, chestnut, and locust,) when planted upon declivities, may often be cut away entirely, with the assurance that the young sprouts, within a season, will more than supply their efficiency. Due care, however, should be taken that such trees be cut either in winter or in early spring, in order to ensure free stooling or (as we say) sprouting. The black birch, which I have named, and which is a very beautiful tree—not as yet, I think, fairly appreciated by our landscapists—will not stool with vigor, if cut after it has attained considerable size ; but the saplings of three or four years, if cut within a foot of the ground, will branch off into a rampant growth of boughs, whose fine spray, even in the winter, is almost equal to its glossy show of summer foliage.

I do not know if I have made my case clear ; but what I have wished has been to guard purchasers, who are really in earnest, against being disturbed or rebuffed by the rough aspect of such country places as commend themselves in other respects. The subjugation of roughness, or rather, the alleviation of it by a thousand little daintinesses of treatment, is what serves chiefly to keep alive interest in a country homestead.

I must say, for my own part, that I enjoy often

for months together some startling defect in my grounds—so deep is my assurance, that two days of honest labor will remove it all, and startle on-lookers by the change.

But let no rural enthusiast hope to up-root all the ill-growth, or to smooth all the roughnesses in a year. He would be none the happier if he could. We find our highest pleasure in conquest of difficulties. And he who has none to conquer, or does not meet them, must be either fool or craven.

Ploughing and Drilled Crops.

ONE of the most striking of those contrasts which arrest the attention of an intelligent agricultural observer, between the tillage of English fields and those of New England, as well as of America generally, is in the matter of plowing. In England, bad plowing is rare; in New England, good plowing is even rarer. Something is to be allowed, of course, for the irregular and rocky surface of new lands, but even upon the best meadow bottoms along our river courses, a clean, straight furrow, well turned, so as to offer the largest possible amount of friable mould for a seed-bed, is a sight so unusual, that in the month of spring travel we might count the number on our fingers. I go still farther, and say—though doubtless offending the patriotic susceptibilities of a great many—that not one American farmer in twenty knows what really good plowing is. Over and over, the wiseacres at the county fairs give their first premiums to the man who, by a little deft handling of the plow, can turn a flat furrow, and who wins his honors by his capacity to hide every vestige of the stubble, and to leave an utterly level surface. But a flat furrow, with ordinary implements, involves a broad cut and a consequent diminution of depth. The perfection of plowing upon sward-land implies, on the contrary, little pyramidal ridgelets of mould, running like an arrow's flight the full length of the field, —all which a good cross-harrowing will break down into fine and even tilth, like a garden-bed. Yet again and again, I have seen such plowing, by Scotch adepts, condemned by the county wise men for its unevenness. The flat furrow is not, indeed, without its uses under certain conditions of the land, and with special objects in view—as, for instance, where, by a fall plowing, one wishes a partial disintegration of the turf, in view of a " turning under " of the whole surface upon the succeeding spring for a crop of roots. This is practised upon the island of Jersey (so famous for its dairy stock) with great success. The sod is " skimmed " (such is their term) in the month of November or December, and with the opening of spring all is turned under by a plow, which, so far as I have observed, is peculiar to that island, and which works ten inches in depth, and requires a team of four horses for its effective use.

I must have a word or two to say here in regard to American plows, which, from the fact that they have received occasional commendatory prizes from foreign committees, have been counted by the sanguine superior to all other implements of the name, and gushing orators have lavished brilliant periods upon our superiority to the world in this branch of agricultural mechanism. Nothing surely can exceed the best American plows in their adaptation to present American needs. They are light, compact, strong, and in rough lands are by half more manageable than the best English implements. But supposing a great reach of well-tilled and perfectly cleared field, and the improved iron Scotch plow will lay a far more true and even furrow with one half the expenditure of manual force. Under such circumstances, the great weight of the Scotch implement, added to its carefully adjusted poise, counts in its favor. We shall gain nothing by denying this and by exaggerating the value of our wooden framework, which has been suggested at once by the cheapness of timber material and by the exigencies of a rough country. Nor have I any manner of doubt that as our culture ripens into seizure of all economic methods, our implement makers will adapt themselves to the new demands with that shrewdness which has thus far been so characteristic of their efforts.

Again, we have no regularly educated plowmen in America. Every man who farms five acres of land thinks he can plow—nay, he is in doubt if anybody in the world can do it better. But good plowing is a thing of education, as much as good preaching, or carpentering, or shoemaking, or writing. Nothing but experience gives the final and effective *vis manutigii.* With the wonderful division of labor in all old countries, every agricultural laborer has his special province and domain of work. And it is quite absurd to suppose that a man who plows only a month out of the twelve can have anything like that due knowledge of the craft, which one acquires by handling the plow-stilts every day, for a hundred days in succession. It is quite true that under a European sky—whether of Belgium, France, or England—tillage can be carried on far into the winter, and that, therefore, there is more occasion that a man be educated for the special office of plowing. But whatever occasion may be, the fact remains the same that, while in Belgium and in Great Britain there is an annual crop of apprentices to the plow, in America there is none. Every man who can use a hoe or a pitch-fork is supposed to

be a competent tailsman for the plow. The result is
—execrably bad work. And I would respectfully
suggest as a subject to which the newly inaugurated
Agricultural Colleges may fitly turn a portion of their
attention, the indoctrination of a certain number of
ambitious young farmers (every fall time) into the
merits of good plowing. I have not, indeed, the
slightest idea that the purveyors of this Congressional agricultural charity would, in most instances,
be capable of giving the requisite instruction, but
they might avail themselves of the offices of here
and there a Scotch farmer who would be competent
to fulfil the trust, and there are always young Americans willing to learn.

Another noticeable feature in European field management, which contrasts strongly with much of
our helter skelter planting, is the almost universal
adoption of the drill system in the culture of all hoed
crops, by virtue of which fertilizing material is applied directly to the plants, and the same distributed
—by a transverse plowing the succeeding season—for
the benefit of the cereal which comes next in rotation. It may be questionable if our corn crop (maize)
will not succeed best under so-called " hill " culture,
and with a broadcast application of manure, since it
is a gross and wide feeder, and demands full flow of
sun and air ; but in respect to most other hoed crops

6

there can be no doubt of the superior economy, as
well as the more orderly appearance of the drill
system.

Take for instance our ordinary crop of potatoes,
(and I think the details of its management were never
before subject of discussion in a similar context;) four
out of ten patches of this worthy esculent, are, in
New England soil, put down in wavy lines of hills—
irregular in distance, slatternly in culture, and yet
involving per bushel a far larger expense for tillage
and harvesting, than if dressed, planted, cleaned, and
earthed up according to some system which would
demand trim lines, even distances, and a complete
shading of the whole ground in the season of their
most rampant growth. Perhaps I shall not be counted
too intolerably practical, if I indicate the actual
method of procedure which has been sometimes followed under my own observation. We will suppose
that a good surface of sward-land (requiring a lift by
reason of its weediness) is turned over lightly, (and
flatly, if you please,) in the month of October. Nothing offers better pabulum for potatoes, or indeed
almost any crop, than decaying turf. In April the
raw surface is levelled with a light Scotch harrow,
and thereupon all is turned under seven inches by the
best plow at command with three horses abreast;
(two will weary of the work.) After this the harrow

is put on again, up and down, and across. There is no fear of harrowing too much. This being accomplished, and the manure disposed (since March) in huge heaps at either end of the field, three deep furrows are opened at, say, two to three rods apart, by a plowman who can drive his furrow across as straight as the flight of an arrow. Immediately upon the opening of the first, the cart follows, and two men strew the open furrow with the half-rotted manure. Another hand follows with a sprinkling of guano and plaster : and still another follows to drop the seed. Upon this the plowman laps a furrow in way of cover : two furrows follow as in ordinary plowing, and every fourth one is treated as we have described with ample dressing and seed. Three series of furrows being opened at the start, permit the plowman to go his rounds without interfering with the planting and dressing. When the whole field is gone over after this system it has simply the appearance of a thoroughly plowed surface. Nothing more is done until the young shoots begin to appear ; at this time the Scotch harrow is put on, and the land completely weeded and levelled, little or no harm being done by this procedure to the starting crop. The whole field has thus the evenness and the cleanness of a garden. Three weeks later, especially if the season be favorable to weed growth, it may be necessary to go be-

tween the rows—now most distinctly and luxuriantly
marked with tufts of green—with the cultivator; and
no future culture is needed until the "earthing-
up" process is accomplished with a double-mould-
board plow. This done, the crop takes care of itself
until harvesting time; no hand hoe, or further culture
being essential. I venture to say that the cost per
bushel is twenty per cent. less than that by the ordinary, hap-hazard hand tillage. In addition to this
there is the delight to the eye of trim rows of luxuriant foliage, interlacing by degrees, and covering the
whole surface with a rich mat of green. If the
experts in the growth of this old esculent—whether
in Maine or on the Bergen flats—have any fault to
find with the method, I will be a patient listener.

Roads and Shade.

I LEAVE potatoes and their culture for a further
consideration of the more striking contrasts between European and American landscape. Not the
least noticeable of these contrasts springs from the
vast difference in the outlay and treatment of the
public roads. A neat and well-ordered public road
in any of the rural districts of America is altogether
exceptional. Throughout Great Britain a slatternly
and ill-kept one is most rare. There is no particular

reason why a cross-country road for farm traffic only should have the width of a village street; yet one uniform turnpike rule of breadth seems to have prevailed in the laying down of all country thoroughfares in America: of course, did the disposition exist, it would by no means be so easy a matter to keep a rambling highway of forty or fifty feet in width, in such orderly condition as a narrower one which would amply suffice for the traffic. Neither towns nor turnpike companies, who mostly have American roads in charge, have any system in their management or any regard for appearances. Exception is to be made in favor of a few public-spirited townships (in Massachusetts mostly) which have taken this matter boldly in hand and encouraged order and thrift by wholesome regulations in regard to encroachments upon the highway, and the judicious planting of trees. For the most part, however, American highroads, throughout the rural districts, offer to the eye two great slovenly stretches of land, cumbered with stones, offal, wood-yards, and gaping with yellow chasms of earth, from which, every spring-time and autumn, a few shovelfuls of clay are withdrawn to patch the road-bed which lies between. Under such conditions the utmost neatness and regularity which the farmer may bestow upon his fields and crops lose half their effect, and the landscape lacks that completed charm

which regales the eye along the rural by-roads of
England.

While town authorities continue to be appointed
for their political aptitude, it is useless to hope for
any mending of such defects, or for any deliberate
scheme of improvement. The most that can be done
is by the combination of adjoining proprietors, in
which they will have little to hope from the coöpera-
tion of any town board of advisers. As an instance
in point—I have repeatedly offered to undertake full
charge of the half-mile of highroad leading through
farm lands of my own, guaranteeing a more serviceable
condition than the road has yet known, and a diminution of cost to the town of at least twenty per
cent., yet the proposition is ignored. The selectmen
would lose their little private jobbing in way of
repairs, and some future board might annul any such
disorderly and unheard of contract.

I have alluded to the planting of trees along highways—a practice which many towns have favored by
public action, and one contributing largely to the
enjoyment of a summer's drive, as well as adding to
the inviting aspect of our country villages. The same
practice obtains along the great public highways of
France, but not so generally in England where the
sunshine is not so common or so fierce as to call for
special protection. Even the country houses of Great

Britain are by no means so shaded as our own ; and the most considerable piles of buildings, such as Eaton Hall, Blenheim, Dalkeith, and Burghley House, have hardly a noticeable tree within stone's throw of their walls. The flower patches, and coppices of shrubbery approach more nearly, and to the garden fronts of those magnificent homes you walk through walls of blooming shrubs. But the full flow of the sunshine upon the window is a thing courted. Allowing for all difference in climate, I think there may be a question if we do not err in this country by over-much shading. A cottage in a wood is a pretty subject for poetry, but it is apt to be uncomfortably damp. And there are village streets with us so embowered that scarce a ray of sunshine can play fairly upon the roofs or fronts of the village houses, from June to October. A summer's life under such screen cannot contribute to the growth of roses in the cheeks any more than to the growth of roses at the door. There is no provision against agues—whether moral or physical— like a good flow of sunshine.

In the establishment of new country houses with us I often observe infinite pains bestowed upon the elaboration of flower-patches, and banks of shrubbery within enjoyable distance of the door, while in the midst of them, or at such little remove as works the same result, a great array of shade trees is planted.

After only a few years, these gross feeders have seized upon all the available plant-food within reach, and with the great lusty boughs of the maples waving over his cherished parterres, the proprietor is amazed at the shrinkage of his flower-growth. It should be fairly understood that about a densely shaded doorstep, the conditions of vigorous and healthful flower-growth can never be maintained.

But far worse, and more to be deprecated than a starvation of the flowers in the immediate neighborhood of a country house, is the starvation of the turf; yet in many of the old established village yards, and about many suburban homes where the fancy for dense overhanging shade has had full sway, even the grasses maintain a doubtful livelihood, and their place is taken by the wild mosses. It may be laid down, I think, as a safe rule, and of universal application in our Northern latitudes, that wherever shade immediately contiguous to the house is too dense for the vigorous growth of the ordinary lawn grasses, it is too dense for proper conditions of health; and I would recommend to the invalid tenants of such a house—in place of nostrums—the axe.

Of course, we can hardly venture to expose our whole frontage to the sun, in the generous way in which the British country liver is wont to do; but *sunshine on the roof* should, I think, be religiously guarded, whatever may become of our old favorites, the trees.

There is another condition of English country life—aside from the climate—which admits of a freer play of sunshine than we may be disposed to admit : it lies in the fact that British houses, whether of brick or stone, are thick-walled (covered, many times, with lichens, if not ivy), and so ward off very effectually the fiercest blasts of July. The thatched roofs of Devon and of Somerset are an even greater protection from the sun.

English and American Hedging.

ANOTHER striking subject of contrast between British and American country road-side, is offered by the numberless array of live hedges which belong to the former, and which probably for generations to come will be wanting in America. In the best-cultivated districts of England, however, hedges are rapidly losing favor for the partition of arable lands, as engrossing too much space, stealing somewhat from the productive capacity of the soil, and offering shelter for noxious weeds. The system of soiling is moreover doing away with the necessity for them, and such ground-feeding as is permitted, is more closely and economically controlled by the

6*

adoption of movable hurdles. The clearing up of those old lines of hawthorn may give delight to the agricultural eye, but the lover of the picturesque will lament their destruction. The cumbrous hedge-rows, too, of Devon and of the Channel Isles (huge dykes of earth with hedge and trees springing from their top) are yielding to the demands of new and progressive culture. I recall many a loitering of a summer's day between these huge banks of green, within sound of the Dart, or of the Exe, or of the beat of the water in *La Fret*—the primroses dotting the close sward, the hedges shutting out the light, the scattered boles wound round with cloaks of ivy, the scant, scraggy limbs interlacing above, and a constant moisture upon the macadamized way, giving life to little truant mats of mosses. But near to the centres of travel and improvement, all these delightful old ridgy banks of moss, and earth, and hedges, and trees, have disappeared. The keen tenants, with the permission of the landlords, are hunting them down in the retired districts. And no wonder; they occupied full twenty feet in width; every rod of them shaded a good perch of grain land; they offered capital breeding places for scores of rabbits. But though a great change is going on in this respect, as well as in the removal of many of the hedges which mark the interior divisions of the farms, the border lines, and

the way-side still show, throughout the month of
April, that wondrous wealth of white hawthorn bloom
which is so associated in the thoughts of all with
English rural landscape. Not always trim, it is true,
are the hawthorn hedges ; not without an occasional
interlacing of rampant brambles ; not without some
stray sapling of other growth cropping out, and
lording it over the line of hedge ; but gnarled, stiff,
strong, waving with the undulations of the hills,
twining with the curves of the road-way—unbroken,
save by here and there a stile or a cumbrous farm-
gate—with a fine spray of interlacing branchlets from
ground to top—white, and noisy with bees in all the
season of bloom—green, and wavy, and flowing in
the flush of the summer's growth—carrying their red
haws through all the early winter, and when the light
snows (as they do, rare times) veil the ground, showing their creeping lines of brown up the hills, and
athwart the hills, and in soldierly array flanking every
country by-road.

When I think of those long billows of green skirting the paths, and look upon my prosaic posts and
rails, it seems to me plain enough that a great bit of
the warp upon which have been woven so many of
the charming rural pictures in British art and song,
is forever wanting to us here. Fancy a trim line of
posts running across the clayey ground of one of

Gainsborough's landscapes! Fancy old Walton sitting under the "rails" for a little chit-chat with his blooming milk-maid! Fancy Milton planting his

> Russet lawns and fallows gray,
> Where the nibbling flocks do stray,

under the lee of a well-morticed rail-fence!

Yet, poetry apart, we shall probably keep by our timber fences for many generations to come in America; first, because, in most parts of the country, it is good economy to do so; and next, because we have as yet no hedge-plant which can thoroughly make good the place of the hawthorn in England.

We are able to grow the hawthorn indeed; but it must be done daintily. It will never bear the rough usage which its ordinary use as a hedge-plant for farm purposes involves. The same is true to an equal extent of the buckthorn, which, in addition, has the bad habit of dying in many of our hard winters; and both these thorns are liable to the attacks of insects (far more pestiferous with us, it would seem, than in Europe), which seriously abridge their use. The white-willow, so trumpeted by bagmen throughout the country is thoroughly a humbug. It is indeed sadly derogatory to the good sense of our rural population that pretenders could ever foist a claim in favor of a willow, of any known habit of growth, upon their acceptance. The osage orange in certain portions of the West, and of the Southwest, promises to be very effective. It starts late in the spring, but holds its foliage until the frost withers it. In the extreme North, and in the Northeast, its shoots are liable to be winter-killed, and its own rampant growth is also against it, as an economic plant for hedging. For effective treatment it requires two or three clippings in the year. This is more, we fancy, than the holders of Western prairie farms will be willing to bestow. After mature years it may possibly show a more tractable disposition in this respect. The honey-locust has been adopted in many quarters, and has its sturdy advocates. But it is open to the same objection of a too luxuriant growth on congenial soils, and of the still more odious objection of a disposition to " sucker," or send up shoots from the roots at a long remove from the parent stem.

The barberry (*Berberis vulgaris*) is strongly commended by many, but it has never yet had, so far as I am aware, fair field trial. A strong objection to it appears to me to lie in the fact that, like the willow, it never inclines to branch from near the root. It sends up indeed a great number of shoots; but shoots of this kind, growing parallel, and showing few leaflets, or little side-spray, can never make a compact, or even a graceful hedge. The old-fashioned farmers of the East have still another objection, as firmly cherished as any dogma they listen to on Sunday, to wit,—the barberry "blasts the rye." This faith is indeed so firmly and persistently cherished that I have been disposed to look for the source of it in some tribe of aphides peculiar to the barberry, which by juxtaposition may transfer its labors to the cereal.

The native white-thorn remains—and it has always seemed to me that with proper nursing, education, and development, much might be made of this as a hedge-plant. The hornbeam, also, of our forests, is a small tree, of profuse spray, bearing the shears admirably ; but, so far as I know, never as yet adopted on a large scale for hedges. The green walks of the gardens of Versailles demonstrate amply what its European congener will suffer in way of clipping.

In the way of evergreen hedge-plants we have nothing to ask for from the nurserymen of Great Britain. Both the arbor-vitæ and the hemlock spruce are admirably adapted to the purpose. The beauty of this latter nothing can exceed, particularly in the season of its first growth (early June), when its flossy light green tufts hang over it like a great shower of golden bloom. The arbor-vitæ is perhaps more manageable, and certainly less impatient of removal ; but it can never become so effective. The Norway spruce is also admirably adapted to hedge uses, and will bear (if *treated early*) the closest clipping of the shears. The grand error in its employment hitherto has been in allowing it to gain some three or four feet in height before resorting to the clipping process.

In fact, the general failure of our hedge experiments throughout the country—whether for service or ornamentation—may be summed up in one word, a lack of care. Farmers have bought hedge-plants by the thousand, and plowing a single furrow or two along the lines of their fields, have set them down under the absurdly ill-founded opinion, that thenceforward they would take care of themselves. But the young and tender hedge-plant, like the young growth of corn, needs culture. And the man who is too indolent or too short-sighted to bestow it, will surely never reap any considerable reward. It is amazing—the short-sightedness which prevails in this regard, not only with respect to hedging, but orcharding, and tree-planting of all kinds. I count it as necessary to the vigorous establishment of a newly-set tree or shrub, that all foreign growth should be kept away from an inclosing circle of from two to four feet radius, as to bestow the like attention upon a hill of corn or of melons. The little fibrous rootlets, such as give nursing to the transplanted stock, are as impatient of any robbery of those sources of sustenance, which find their way through the ground, as the annual plants. We should have heard far less lament in this country over the failure of hedges if there had been more considerate treatment of them during the early years of their establishment.

If this careful nurture be requisite in respect to stock from the nurseries, it is ten-fold more important with respect to young plants transferred directly from the forest. Scores of failures I have known on the part of those, who—being delighted with the appearance of some lusty screen of hemlocks—have undertaken to rival it by direct transfer of the wild growth to some lean streak of plowed land, and have thereafter left the shivering field-pensioners to struggle for themselves. The half would very likely or very properly die; the rest maintain only a meagre semblance of life, and show none of that rampant vigor which is essential to the beauty of a hedge. Indeed, except in fully kept garden-ground, I would advise no one to make this direct transfer. A season or two in the nursery rows develops an enormous stock of rootlets, and thereafter, with ordinary care, every plant may be counted on.

I doubt very greatly the serviceableness of any of the evergreen hedges for farm purposes; both the hemlock and Norway spruce, for full development, demand considerable width, more than would be con-

sistent with farm-economy, and much greater than
would be ordinarily accorded to the hawthorn; besides which, they are by no means proof against the
mischievous forays of cattle, who love nothing better
than to tangle their horns in a wall of soft green and
twist away the branchlets. The thorn-bearing shrubs
are by no means so inviting to their ventures of this
sort.

I have not spoken of the holly—of which many
charming hedges are to be found on English estates
—because the British plant has not proved itself
wholly equal to our climate, and the American holly
(besides being somewhat inferior in glossiness and
density of foliage) has not yet been commonly introduced even among nurserymen. In the way, however, of leafy screens for garden parterres and terraces, I have great hopes of what may yet be accomplished with our Rhododendron and Kalmia latifolia.
The lank, lean habit of this latter under its ordinary
transplanting is no measure of its capacity for making
a full, rounded, dense wall of green. Whoever has
wandered over high-lying pasture-lands of New
England which have recently been cleared of their
forest growth, and has seen the wanton, luxuriant,
crowded tufts of Kalmia shooting from the old roots,
can form some measure of the capacity of the shrub
for good screen effects. The lank growth, too, of the

Rhododendron in a few shaded swamp-lands where it
finds its *habitat* in New England, is no indication of
what may be done with it under fairer conditions of
growth.

And this mention of the laurel family (I like that
old popular naming of these shrubs) reminds me of
the screens and coppices which greet the eye so often
in English gardens and in English landscape. It is
quite possible that with our climate, we can never
equal their variety. The Bay, the Spanish laurel, the
Laurestina, will very likely be fastidious in adjusting
themselves to our winters. But with our narrow-
leaved laurel, our Latifolia, our Rhododendrons, we
can pile up a wealth of glossy green against the
northern sides of our gardens, which even the best
British farmers might envy. Add to these our
spruces (hemlock and others), our white pine (Stro-
bus), for background, and we have nothing to covet.

But if we have nothing to covet, we have very
much to learn in the adjustment of our leafy screens.
Over and over I observe some ambitious gentleman
(at the hands of his gardener) attempting to establish
a protective coppice, and after careful and expensive
preparation of the ground (there is nothing lacking
on that score), placing his rare evergreens where they
will be presently overgrown and lost, or putting out
his Rhododendrons where they will have no room for

full and rounded development, or crowding his spruces, and his Deodars, and Scotch pines, so that in a few years there is but a thicket of close-growing boles—offering no shelter from the wind, and graded by no forecast of the relative measure of growth. Or if, by accident, the planting be judicious, there follows none of that resolute trimming and bold use of the axe, under which only a protective group of trees can be made to maintain its rounded symmetry and its artistic agreement with the landscape.

Indeed, we are as yet only beginning to learn what the real worth of screening banks of foliage are to fruit, to gardens, and even to grain-fields. It is doubtful if it be not the last lesson—but certainly not the least important—which is learned in ornamental or economic arboriculture.

Village Greens.

IF I enter a little quiet plea for the old-fashioned Village Greens, I hope I shall not be decried by the reformers. Village Greens are not quotable at the "Board." Our friend of the Avenue cannot dash through them with his equipage. There are no patches of choice exotics upon the village green— possibly not even a serpentine path; no fountain, I am sure, that shows the spasmodic gush of the city

fountains.   And yet the name—Village Green, is,
somehow, tenderly cherished; it rallies to my thought
a great cycle of rural memories belonging to song, to
childhood, to story and to travel—wherein I see, in
bountiful procession, broad-armed elms, dancing peas-
ants, flocks of snowy geese, shadows of church
spires, boys with satchels, bonfires of fallen leaves,
militia " trainings," and some irate Betsey Trotwood,
making a soldierly dash at intruding donkeys.   It is
quite possible that these ill-assorted memories may
confound public and private Greens, as well as English and American, but all have their spring in that
good old name of the Village Green.   I hope that it
is not a strange name, and that it will never grow
strange while grass is green, and villages are founded.

In old days of stage-coach travel, one came, after
a tedious, lumbering drag over hills, and through
swampy flats, (where, if season favored, wild grapevines, or white azalias, tossed their rich fragrance into
coach windows,) upon some lifted plateau of land,
where the white houses shone among trees, flanking a
level bit of greensward, and geese grazed the common; and where was a whipping-post, may be—possibly a decaying pair of oaken stocks, and a court-
house with its belfry.   I do not think such old village
commons of New England, (and I suspect they were
rarely to be seen in other parts of the country,) were

ever very nicely kept. The geese cropped the grass
short, to be sure ; but geese are not a tidy animal ;
the pool, too—if any pondlet of water broke the
surface of the level—was apt to show the stamp of
adventurous hoofs and a muddy margin ; for all this,
however, such eyelets of green space in the centre of
country towns, around which and upon which all the
gayety and cheer of the settlement might disport
itself, were very charming. I do not know but I
would rejoice to see the village stocks brought into
use again, for the sake of the broad common where
they stood : certain it is, that if they were ever serviceable (I speak of the stocks), they would be serviceable now. I think I could mention a fat grocer
or two, and two or three editors, or more, who
would look well—sitting in the stocks. And as for
the whipping-posts, who would not rejoice to see
their revival, provided only he could name the incum-
bents of the post-office ?

But I have no right to speak of the Village Green
as wholly a thing of the past, although such symbols
of order and discipline as the stocks and the whipping-post have gone by.

Travellers rarely meet with them, it is true ; but
we do not travel by stage-coach nowadays. We do
not face the old orderly frontage of quiet, outlying
towns, as we did when we clattered down the main

street to the common and the tavern and the pump. If we travel thitherward, we are thrust into the backsides of towns upon some raw cut of a railway, amid all manner of *debris* and noisome smells. Now I suppose that old-time villagers took a pride in their common, with its stately trees—in their court-house, their breadth and neatness of high-road, as being the objects which must of necessity fasten the regard of those from the outside world who paid their town a visit. The two deacons who lived opposite, would never coquette in their door-yards, or fences, for the entertainment of each other, but rather for the admiration of the public, which must needs pass their doors. But yet—and it is a curious fact in the history of public taste—in these times, when old villages are disembowelled by the railway, and all their showiness turned inside out, there seems very little regard paid to the observation of that larger public which is hurtling by every day in the cars.

The former traveller along the high-road, was cautiously placated with orderly palings, neat door-yards, an array of grass and flowering shrubs, with a church in imposing position ; but the larger public that now visits the locality is greeted with a terrific array of backsides, of lumbering styes, disorderly fences, and no token that the village world is cognizant of their presence, or careful of their judgment. Of course, the habit of a village life cannot be changed so quickly as a railway cutting is made—the new world of progress may be upon them before they are aware ; but when actually present, why not meet it with something of the old tidiness and pride ?

Can any rural philosopher explain us this matter ? Does the whirl of the world into sudden sight of all our disorderly domesticity, break up self-respect, and weaken faith in appearances ?

Here, and there indeed, I observe one who newly paints his rear door, and trims his hedges, and plants his arbors, and gravels his walks, so as to impress favorably the new passers-by of the rail ; but for one who shows this solicitude respecting the new public, a dozen keep to a stolid indifference, and living with their faces the other way, leave the pigs and a mangy dog to squeal and bark a reception to the world of the railway.

I cannot quite explain this. Most of us love to carry a name for respectability and good order and decency, and do not like to be discovered kicking the cat or indulging in any similar personal gratifications or wants. It is true we do not know one in a thousand of the ten thousand who hurtle past our homestead ; but how many of those who make up the body of that public opinion, in the eye of which we wish to live with decency and order, do we know ?

What all this may have to do with the topic of Village Greens, may be not quite clear to the reader; but I will try and develop its bearings. All the lesser towns through which or near to which a railway passes, have virtually changed face; they confront the outside world no longer upon their embowered street or quiet common, but at the " station." *There* lies the point of contact, and there it must remain until the mechanicians shall have devised some airy carriage which shall drop visitants from the clouds upon the threshold of the cosy old hostelrie.   There being thus, as it were, a new focal point of the town life, it wants its special illustration and adornment. The village cannot ignore the railway : it is the common carrier ; it is the bond of the town with civilization ; it lays its iron fingers upon the lap of a hundred quiet valleys, and steals away their tranquillity like a ravisher.

What then ? Every village station wants its little outlying Green to give character and dignity to the new approach.   Is there any good reason against this ?   Nay, are there not a thousand reasons in its favor ?   In nine out of ten wayside towns, such space could be easily secured, easily held in reserve, easily made attractive ; and if there were no room for a broad expanse of sward, at least there might be planted some attractive copse of evergreens or shrub-

bery, to declare by graceful type the rural pride of
the place. He would be counted a sorry curmudgeon
who should allow all visitors to make their way to
his entrance-hall, through wastes of dust and piles of
offal ; cannot the corporate authorities of a town be
taught some measure of self-respect, and welcome the
outside world with indications of orderly thrift, blooming and carrying greeting to the very threshold of
the place ?

First impressions count for a great deal—whether
in our meeting with a woman, or with a village. Slip-
shoddiness is bad economy in towns, as is people.
Every season there is a whirl of citizens, tired of city
heats and costs, traversing the country in half hope
of being wooed to some summer home, where the
trees and the order invite tranquillity and promise
enjoyment. A captivating air about a village station
will count for very much in the decision. There will
be growth, to be sure, in favored localities, in spite
of disorder. I could name a score of little towns
along the line of the New Jersey and Erie and Hudson Railways, with their charming suburban retreats
near by, to which the occupant must wade his way
through all manner of filthiness and disorderly *debris*,
making his landing, as it were, in the very dung-heap
of the place, and smacking with a relish, it would
seem, these prefatory incidents of his country home.

7

Is there no mending this? Are selectmen all swine or swineherds? Do city residents count for nothing or care for nothing in the health or air of the railway centre of the towns of their adoption? Dram-shops, and oyster-shops, and as dirty land-offices, will, doubtless, in the present civilization, have position somewhere; but must they needs be foisted upon the area about the village station? Is no redemption possible? Must we always confront the town with its worst side foremost? Suppose for a moment that the old Village Green were translated to the neighborhood of the station, or a companion spot of rural attractiveness established there, around which the waiting equipages might circle in attendance—suppose a pleasant shade of elms spreading itself upon that now dusty area—suppose the corporate authorities keenly alive to the aspect which their town and its approaches may wear in the eye of the world which looks on, and forms its judgment every day by thousands—suppose an inviting inn, duly licensed, swings its sign under some near bower of trees, will all this count nothing toward the growth, the reputation, the dignity of a country locality? I know I am writing in advance of the current practice in these respects; but I am equally sure that I am not writing in advance of the current practice fifty years hence, if only the schools are kept open. The reputation of a town for order, for neatness, for liberality, or taste, is even now worth something, and it is coming to be worth more, year by year.

Railway Gardening.

I HAVE alluded to the railway station and its surroundings, because it seems to me that—in the lessons of public taste which are being read from time to time by those competent to teach on such topics—this new junction of the world with country localities is being sadly overlooked. Where indeed can there be a hopeful opening for any æsthetic teaching, if this inoculation and grafting-point of the business world with the world ruminant and rural, is allowed to fix, with all its ugly swell of swathing bandages and pitch and mud, uncared for?

The question of proprietorship might give some difficulty, but it is one whose difficulties would vanish, if only the corporate authorities of town and road could be brought to act in harmony. Nor is there any reason in the economies of the matter why they should not. The road secures a limited area for the establishment of its station, and some outlying grounds, in most cases, to guard against future contingencies—which grounds usually rest in a most

forlorn condition, giving refuge, may be, to condemned sleepers or wreck of wheels—possibly ten-
anted by some burly night porter, who thrusts his
stove-pipe through the roof of a dismantled car—
showing just that disarray, in short, which declares
no pride or proof of ownership. If there chance to
be any half-filled pits upon the premises, enterprising
Celtic citizens of the neighborhood count them good
spots into which to shoot their garbage. All this
the town authorities regard as a matter which con-
cerns only the distinguished corporation of the road.
Thus, between them, the most unkempt and noisome
wilderness about the half of such of our country
towns as are pierced by railways is apt to lie in the
purlieus of the station. Yet railway directors are,
some of them, professing Christians, and so are town
authorities—at times. What now if these good people (*hæc verbi magnificentia !*) would lay their heads
together to compass what might prove a gain to the
town thrift, and so indirectly to the road, without
positive loss to either? What if the town were to
extend the area of the corporation lands at its own
cost, so far as to establish a little bowling green, that
should give piquant welcome to every stranger, and
grow to be an object of town pride? What if care
of all grounds adjoining the station should be subject
to some custodian, bound to control them after some

simple prescribed rules of order, whose fulfilment
would work an economy to the company, and add a
grace to that portion of the village?

I cannot help recalling to mind here some of
those charming wayside stations upon the Continent
—in France, Germany, and Switzerland—where the
station-master is also manager of a blooming garden
(the property of the company), which he manages
with such tender care that the blush of the roses and
the muffled scent of the heliotropes come to me again
as I read the name of the station upon the Guide
Book. And yet those French, those German, those
Swiss corporators, who encourage their station-masters to such handicraft, are shrewd money men.
They find their account in all this; they like to make
their roads attractive; the way-side villagers encourage them in it to the full bent of their capacity.

In one quarter (among those stations of which I
speak, but I cannot now just say where) I was pro-
voked into special inquiries: "This nice treatment
involved a great bill of expense doubtless?"

"Very great care—grand labor!"

"It must make a heavy bill for the company to
foot?"

"*Pardon, monsieur*, the work is mine and the
gain is mine."

"Not very much, it is to be feared."

" *Pardon* " again ; the station-master (it was only
an out of the way country station) has sold enough
of bouquets to passing travellers to establish his boy
at a *pension :* he hopes everything for his boy.   The
story gave a new fragrance to the roses, and to the
marguerites which he handed me.

Now, I am afraid our station-masters, whether in
Massachusetts or along the Hudson, will not be capable of making themselves good florists at a bound ;
but yet the hint has its value.   What objection can
there possibly be to the careful culture of such strips
of land as come within the jurisdiction of every station-master upon our iron roads ?   In not infrequent
instances he has the lea of some deep cutting for
shelter ; he has the eyes of an observing crowd (who
are debarred from pilfering) for an incentive ; he may
have his thousand customers for floral offerings every
summer's day.   Could not the townsfolk aid, with
prudent foresight, in any such diversion of the waste
strips of railway lands ?   The area in gross is not
small ; miles upon miles of bank cutting, of marsh
land, of embankment, of green level, each one of
which will grow its own crop after methods which a
wealthy and intelligent railway corporation might
surely direct.   Osiers upon the low lands, shrubs
upon the raw cuttings (binding them against wash),
grasses upon the verdant lands, a flame of flowers

around every station. Does anybody doubt that this
thing is to be in the years to come? Does anybody
doubt (who believes in progress) that some day the
directors, now so stolid and indifferent, will make a
merit of it, and take a pride in pointing out their
horticultural successes upon their league-long strips
of garden?

One very great advantage in that nice culture
which is to be observed about many of the British
and Continental railway stations lies in the fact, that
the culture and its success are submitted every day to
thousands of eyes. What you or I may do very suc-
cessfully, and in obedience to the best laws of taste
and vegetable physiology on some back country property, may really benefit the public very little, for the
reason that the public will never put eye upon it;
but what our horticultural friend at a railway station
may do (if done well) is of vastly more profit. It is
in the way of being seen; it is in the way of being
seen of those who are not immediately engrossed
with other care than the easy care of travel; it gives
suggestions to them in their most accessible moods.
To this day I think I have fixed in my mind many a
little gracefully arranged parterre of bloom, only
petunias and pansies and four o'clocks, may be, which
I saw only a few moments on some day, now far
gone, in other latitudes, and of which the scant

memorial is but some jotting down upon a foreign
note-book, followed by a scant pencilling of the actual
adjustment, so far as the brief stay allowed of transcript.

The chemists tell us that the air of cities and their
neighborhood is richer in available nitrogen (in shape
of ammonia or nitric acid) than the air of the country,
by reason of the outpourings from so many chimney-
tops, and the attendant processes of combustion. May
not the cinders and the fine ash and the gases
evolved from a great highway of engines always
puffing and smoking in the lower strata of the atmosphere contribute somewhat, and that not inconsider-
ably, to the plants found along the lines of such highway? I am not aware that experiment has as yet
determined anything on this score; and whatever
such determination might be, it is certain that abundant sources of fertilization might be secured at every
country station, sufficient amply to equip an investing garden. Upon the oldest roads very much could
be done still in way of this charming investiture, and
in way of the adjoining bowling-green, under encour-
agement of the town, or of neighboring property-
holders; and upon all new lines of railway, wherever
new stations are established, everything could be
done. To make a township attractive, the approach
to it must be attractive. Will not our Western

burghers who are interested in the growth of townships make a note of this fact, and do somewhat for
the benefit of the coming generation as well as for
their own advantage, by so ordering the establishment of railway stations as to determine and insure
the attractive features I have named?

Landscape Treatment of Railways.

WHILE upon this subject of railway gardens
and culture, I have a word to say to all who
have lands adjoining upon these iron clamps of our
present civilization. A great accession of responsi-
bility comes to them by reason of their position. A
slatternly wall, a disgraceful method of tillage, a reeking level of undrained land, in far away districts, may
corrupt but few young farmers and confirm them in
bad practices, by reason of their isolation. But upon
a great highway of travel, where a thousand eyes
measure the shortcomings day by day, a good or a
bad example will have a hundred-fold force.

It would seem, indeed, as if a shrewd business
economy would commend care and nicety of tillage.
The adventurous hair-dressers and fabricators of a
myriad nostrums, paint their advertisements on the
rocks; what better advertisement of a farm or garden,

7*

or nursery or wood or meadow, than such equipment of them all with the best results of thorough care and culture, as to fasten the eye and pique investigation? I know a suburban architect who, by the harmonics and order of a homestead, in full view of a thousand travellers a day, has doubled his business. So the grace of a parterre or the artistic arrangement of a terrace or a walk in the eye of so many, may make the reputation of a gardener. Every dweller, indeed, upon a line of railway, has a reputation to make or lose in all that relates to his treatment of ground, whether as woodland, farm, or garden.

If the homestead be so near the clatter of the trains as to give too great exposure of the domestic offices, good taste, as well as the quiet which most country-livers enjoy, will suggest a planting out of the line of traffic by thickets of evergreens; and these, by their careful adjustment, and occasional openings for a glimpse at the more attractive features of the situation, will themselves give such a place a character. If, however, the house be so remote as to admit of all desired seclusion about the dooryard and to yield only distant views of the trail of carriages whirling up their white curls of steam, a mere hedge may mark the dividing-line, or some simple paling, and the lands between, whether in lawn or tillage, may be so ordered as to greet the eye of every intelligent traveller, or impress upon him such rural lessons as every adjoining proprietor should make it a virtue to teach.

When a farm or country-seat is traversed by a deep cutting for the railway bed—so deep as to forbid any extended side views—a tasteful proprietor may still mark his lands noticeably, and well, by arranging—in concert with the railway officials—an easily graded slope upon either side of the cutting, which, by a few simple dressings, shall be brought into a grassy surface—telling a good story for the flats above, and showing upon their extreme height a skirting hedge-row or coppice, or possibly the trellis of some rustic paling, blooming with flowers, and (if convenience of pathway require it) stretching upon either side of a bridgelet, across the chasm of the road. Even where such cutting is through cliff, nothing is to forbid the dressing of the higher ledges with a few crimson bunches of columbines, to nod their heads between the eye of the traveller and the sky, and make good report, from their little corners, of the people whose every-day walk skirts the cliffs. If a gradual slope, or terraces, are admissible by the nature of the cutting, it is a question if these may not be made to carry their parterres of flowers, or of blooming shrubs, to give charm to the borders of an estate. I have somewhere seen such slope, whereon

an adventurous nurseryman had given advertisement
of his name and calling by an ingenious arrangement
of his box-borders in gigantic lettering—not, perhaps,
a very legitimate rural decoration, or such as a severe
taste would commend—and yet I cannot but think
that a little trail of fiery flowers, scattered, as it were,
upon a bank of lawn, and spelling out some graceful
name (of the homestead), which should be discernible only one swift moment as the train flashed by,
while to one looking forward or backward, it should
be only a careless ribbon of flowers flecking the green
—I say I can hardly fancy that this would smack of
tawdriness. However this may be, devices there are,
innumerable, for conferring grace upon such sudden
slopes as I have hinted at : a slope to the north will
carry admirably its tufts of rhododendron and of
kalmia, or its confused tangle of hemlocks and Deodar
cedars.

The English ivy, too, will grow admirably in such
situations, upon a ground surface, taking root here
and there, and covering all the lesser inequalities
with its glossy network of leaves. Such condition
of growth, moreover, (trailing over the surface of the
ground,) insures protection by snows ; or, if that be
wanting, a thin coating of litter spread over the
creeper will be an ample defence. The ivy is winter-
killed, not so much by extreme cold, as by sudden

alernations of temperature, and exposure of its stiff-
ened leaves to the scalding sunbeams which sometimes belong even to a northern winter. Protection
from the January sun is, I believe, as important as
protection from extreme cold.

Where the railway passes through a country property upon the same general level with a lawn surface
or farm lands, the rules for adjustment—of crops or
of decorative features—so as to carry their best landscape effects, will be comparatively easy. All right
lines—whether of annual crops, hedge-rows, or avenues—will, of a surety, lose effect by being established
parallel to the line of road. At what angle they
should touch upon it, will be best determined by the
nature of the surface, and by the conditions of the
background.

I know that it is the habit of many who control
large estates adjoining railways, to ignore, so far as
possible, this iron neighbor, and to make all their
plans of improvement with a contemptuous disregard
of the travelling observers, who count by thousands,
considering only the few who look on from the old
high-road, or those, still fewer, who have the privilege
of the grounds. But in a republican country, this is
monstrous; monstrous, indeed, in any country where
a man properly reckons his responsibilities to his fellows. If he has conceived new lessons of taste, it is

his duty so to illustrate them as to make them command the acceptance of the multitude. He has no right to ignore the onlook of the world, and be careless if the world condemns or approves.

A high railway embankment traversing the low lands of a country estate, if at a good remove from the homestead, is not so awkward a matter to deal with as might at first be supposed. A few years of well-tended growth in a forest screen may be made to exclude it altogether; but care should be taken lest such screen, by its uniformity, should present the same tame outlines with the embankment itself. To avoid this, the woody plantation should flow down in little promontories of shrubbery upon the flat; it should have its open bays upon the embankment itself, disclosing at intervals a glimpse of the passing trains; and, above all, the bridge or culvert, which keeps good the water-courses of the land, should be distinctly indicated, and might have its simple decorative features.

All this, if picturesque effect only is aimed at: but if it be desirable to utilize such monster embankment, it may be remembered that its shelter, if looking to the south, would almost create a summer climate of its own, and would make admirable lee for the forcing-houses of the gardeners, and for the growth of whatever plants or vegetables crave the first heats of the spring sun. The traveller will recall the " little Provence," in the garden of the Tuileries, where, by the mere shelter of a twelve-foot terrace wall circling around against cool winds, a summer balmi-ness is given to the locality even in winter, and phthi-sical old men and feeble children find their way thither to luxuriate in the sunshine.

If, on the other hand, such embankment flank the north, its shadow will offer capital nursery-ground for the rhododendrons, ivies, and all such plants as are impatient of the free blast of the sun.

And, after all, if these happy accidents of posi-tion and opportunity did not favor such special culture, it should be the duty and the pride of the true artist in land-work to ascertain what other growths would be promoted by exceptional disturbances of surface. The finest and highest triumphs in landscape art are wrought out in dealing with portentous features of ugliness, and so enleashing them with the harmonies of a given plan as to extort admiration.

The railway, with its present bald embankments, and its baldness of all sorts, is a prominent feature in many of our suburban landscapes. It cannot be ignored, and the study must be to harmonize its sweep of level line, its barren slopes, its ugly scars, its deep cuttings, with the order and grace of our fields and homes. Rains and weather-stains and wild growths are doing somewhat to mend the harshness; but a little artistic handling of its screening foliage, and adroit seizure of the opportunities furnished for special culture, will quicken the work. And it is to this end that I have thrown out these hints upon so novel a subject as that of railway gardening.

LAYING OUT OF GROUNDS.

LAYING OUT OF GROUNDS.

Landscape Gardening.

IS it an art or a trade that I propose for discussion? I think it is an art. The backwoodsman would not agree with me; there are many plethoric citizens who would not agree. Good roads, and paths laid where you want them, and plenty of shade trees —is there anything more than this in the laying out of grounds? Is there any *finesse*, any special aptitude requisite, or anything that approaches the domain of art in managing the matter, as such matter should be managed?

I think there is; and that it is an art as yet, in this country, almost in its infancy; and yet an art instinctively appreciated by cultivated persons wherever it declares itself, whether upon a small or a large area.

We have admirable engineers who can lay down an approach road, or other, with easy grades, and great grace—so far as the curves count for grace; and we have gardeners who shall lay down your flower-beds and grounds for shrubbery according to the newest rules, and with great independent beauties in themselves; but it is quite possible that both these classes of workers may fill their designs admirably, and yet steer clear of the great principles of the art I purpose to discuss. It is an art which takes within its purview good engineering and good architectural work, and good gardening, and good farming, if you please; but which looks to their perfect accordance—which dominates, in a sense, the individual arts named, and accomplishes out of the labors of each a congruous and captivating whole.

Good farming, good gardening, good engineering, and good architecture may stand side by side upon a given estate, and yet, for want of due conception of what the landscape really demands for its completed charm, the effect may be incongruous and unsatisfying. Over and over again a wealthy proprietor seeks to supply the somewhat that is lacking by inordinative and cumulative expenditure: he may thus make outsiders wonder and gape; he may also secure a great assemblage of individual beauties; but the charming oneness of effect which shall make his place

an exemplar of taste and a perpetual delight is somehow wanting.

The true art of landscape gardening lies in such
disposition of roadways, plantations, walks, and buildings as shall most effectively develop all the natural
beauties of the land under treatment, without con-
flicting (or rather in harmony) with the uses to which
such lands may be devoted. Thus, in a private estate,
home interests and conveniences must be kept steadily
in view, and these must never be sacrificed for the
production of a pictuesque effect, however striking in
itself. Again, in a public park the same law obtains,
and any good design for such must show great amplitude of roadway, and broad, open spaces for the disport of the multitude. Upon farm-lands, which I
hold to be not without the domain of landscape treatment, there must be due regard to the offices of rural
economy, and the decorative features may be safely
brought out in the shape of gateways, belts of protecting shrubbery, or scattered coppices upon the
pasture-lands. Upon ground entirely level, the range
of possible treatment is, of course, very much limited;
but the true artist in landscape effects can do something even with this; no architect worthy of the
name despairs if he is confined to four walls of even
height; in his own art, if he loves it, he finds decorative resources.

I have alluded to the possibility of artistic land-scape treatment in connection with farm-lands; this opinion is, I am aware, opposed to the traditional theory of the British writers upon the subject; but we are living in advance of a good many traditions of that sort. The Duke of Marlborough keeps the open glades of his park-land short and velvety by his herd of fallow deer. Our wealthy citizen, on the other hand, will probably keep his largest stretch of level land in presentable condition with a Buckeye Mower, and will depend upon the cutting as a winter's baiting for his Alderney heifers; but this will not forbid an occasional group of oaks or maples, or the massing of some graceful shrubbery around an intruding cliff. It will never do, indeed, for us as Americans to sanction the divorce of landscape from our humbler rural intentions—else the great bulk of our wayside will be left without law of improvement. Not only those broad and striking effects which belong to a great range of field and wood, or to bold scenery, come within the domain of landscape art, but those lesser and orderly graces that may be compassed within stone's throw of a man's door. We do not measure an artist by the width of his canvas. The panoramas that take in mountains are well, if the life and the mists of the mountains are in them; but they do not blind us to the merit of a cabinet gem.

I question very much if that subtle apprehension of the finer beauties which may be made to appear about a given locality does not express itself more pointedly and winningly in the management of a three or five acre lawn, than upon such reach of meadow and upland as bounds the view. The watchful care for a single hoary boulder that lifts its seared and lichened hulk out of a sweet level of greensward ; the audacious protection of some wild vine flinging its tendrils carelessly over a bit of wall, girt with a savage hedge-growth—these are indications of an artist feeling that will be riotous of its wealth upon a bare acre of ground. Nay, I do not know but I have seen about a laborer's cottage of Devonshire such adroit adjustment of a few flowering plants upon a window-shelf, and such tender and judicious care for the little matlet of turf around which the gravel path swept to his door, as showed as keen an artistic sense of the beauties of nature, and of the way in which they may be enchained for human gratification, as could be set forth in a park of a thousand acres. Of course, I do not mean to imply that the man who could fill a peasant's rood of ground with charms of shrub or flower, would, by virtue of so humble attainment, be competent to produce the larger effects of landscape gardening. This would, of course, involve a wider knowledge and a different order of experience ; but the eye and the taste, which are the final judges, must be much the same.

Farm Landscape.

IN further reference to the possible connection of landscape art with lands submitted every year to agricultural and economic uses, I propose to examine the matter in detail. If all farm-lands showed only the method of Alderman Mechi's, and his system of pumping dirty water by steam into the middle of any field—to be distributed thence by hose and sprinklers—should prevail, we should have, of course, only flat surfaces and rectangular fields to deal with. But it is safe to say that it will not prevail upon most of our American farms for many years to come; yet it is none the less true that farm-lands are chiefly valued for the crops they will carry, and for the annual return they will make. Are lands under such rule of management susceptible of an æsthetic governance as well? Will treatment with a view to profit, discard of necessity all consideration of tasteful arrangement? I think not, and for reasons among which I may adduce the following: Judicious location of a farm-steading, with a view to profit simply, will be always near the centre of the lands farmed: this is agreeable, moreover, to every landscape-ruling in the matter. The ricks, the chimney, the barn-roofs, the dove-cots, the door-yard, with its skirting array of shrubbery and shade trees,—if only order and neatness belong to them, as good economy would dictate,—form a charming nucleus for any stretch of fields. If there be a stream whose power for mechanical purposes can be made available, economy dictates a location of the farm buildings near to its banks : taste does the same. If there be a hill whose sheltering slope will offer a warm lee from the north-westers, a due regard for the comfort of laborers and of beasts, to say nothing of early garden crops, will dictate the occupancy of such sheltered position by the group of farm buildings : taste will do the same. If such slope has its rocky fastness, incapable of tillage, and of little value for pasture, economy will suggest that it be allowed to develop its own wanton wild growth of forest : a just landscape taste will suggest the same. If there be a broad stretch of meadow or of marsh land, subject to occasional over-flow, or by the necessity of its position not capable of thorough drainage, good farming will demand that it be kept in grass : good landscape gardening will do the same.

Again, such rolling hillsides as belong to most farms of the East, and which by reason of their declivity or impracticable nature are not readily sub-

8

ject to any course of tillage, will be kept in pasture, and will have their little modicum of shade. The good farmer will be desirous of establishing this shade around the brooklet or the spring which waters his herd, or as a sheltering belt to the northward and westward of his lands : the landscapist cannot surely object to this. The same shelter along the wayside is agreeable to all æsthetic laws, and does not surely militate against any of the economies of farming. Indeed, I may remark here, as I have already done in the progress of these pages, that the value of a sheltering belt of trees is not sufficiently appreciated as yet by practical farmers ; but those who are not insensible to the quick spring growth under the lee of a northern garden-fence, will one day learn that an evergreen belt along the northern line of their farms will show as decisive a gain in their fields or their orcharding.

Again, in the disposition of roadways, there is no rule in landscape gardening which is not applicable to a farm. Declivities are to be overcome by the easiest practicable grades, and the curves which will insure this in most landscapes are those which are justified at a glance by the economic eye, as well as by the eye of taste. A straight walk up and down a hill, is a monstrosity in park scenery ; and it is a monstrosity that cannot be found in pasture-lands, where cattle beat their own paths. Even sheep, who are good climbers in search of food, whenever they wend their way to the fold, take the declivities by zigzag, and give us a lesson in landscape art. An ox-team, in worming its way through woodland and down successive slopes, will describe curves which would not vary greatly from the engineering laws of adjustment.

Once more, there are certain special features about a farm-steading, which may be led to contribute largely to landscape effect without violation of economic law. These are the ventilators upon the barn roof (which no good barn should be without), the dove-cots, the chimney-stacks, the ricks (for which a nice thatch is an economy), the Dutch barns, with their pointed roofs and rustic base, the windmill (if one is dependent upon pumps), the orcharding—all which may be made to contribute their quota to an effective landscape, without great violation of the practical aims of the farmer.

I have dwelt upon this point, because I love to believe and to teach that in these respects true taste and true economy are accordant, and that the graces of life, as well as the profits, may be kept in view by every ruralist, whether farmer or amateur. There have been certain *fermes ornées* both in England and France (may be in this country too), which I do not

at all reckon in my estimate of the relations of good
farming to the positive laws of taste. They are play-
farms, upon which it is thought necessary, (however
flat the surface,) to give to the fields all manner of
irregular and curvilinear shapes. Such an arrangement is to every judicious farmer an affront. If a
field takes irregular shape for sufficient reason—in its
surface, or encroachment of cliff, border territory, or
water,—well and good; the farmer can account for
it, and accommodate his labors to it. But if it be a
fantasy merely, which requires him to back his team
and give inequality to his " lands," his common-sense
revolts at it; he sees an empty device that interrupts
his labor and provokes his contempt. The contempt,
I think, any man of true taste will share with him.

There is nothing horrible in a straight line (whatever some gardeners may think) upon flat surfaces.
I am inclined, indeed, to favor strongly the old Dutch
instinct for long clipped avenues, and for the straight
belts of trees along their water-courses, in Holland.
Why should they puzzle themselves with curves,
where no curves were needed? Or over the great
sheep plains of Central France, what mockery it
would have been to conduct a highway (or any other
way for convenience) by the meanderings which
belong so naturally to a highway of Devonshire!

Of course, I speak of landscape here in a large

way. A man may very properly have his door-yard
and garden curvatures upon a plane surface, if they
be accounted for by judicious planting. I have even
seen little hillocks thrown up upon a two-acre patch
of adroitly arranged pleasure-ground which suggested
agreeably larger and more graceful hillocks near by
that were not attainable. But a man who should
undertake the building of a considerable hill in a
level country to relieve the monotony, would very
likely have his labor for his pains. Even the great
tumulus upon the field of Waterloo, upon which the
Belgian lion snuffs the air, had to me always a most
absurd look of impropriety. A group of white head-
stones or a column of marble would have told more
gracefully the story of the Belgian dead. The stupendous rock-work at Chatsworth, again, always appeared to me a most monstrous waste of good honest
material and honest labor. It is very costly and
expensive ; but one of the least of God's cliffs would
overshadow it utterly. Its artificiality cannot cheat
one who knows what rocks are in the fissures of the
hills ; and he looks upon it, at best, with the same
sort of foolish wonderment with which he looks upon
the wooden puppets in the Dutch gardens of Brock.

Thus much I have written to show, so far as I
might, that the small landholder can avail himself
of the laws of the best landscape art, and in virtue

of them can confirm and establish the neatness and order of his fields. There is, indeed, an artificiality about his straight lines of crops, and his rectangular enclosures which does not tempt the painter; but it is an artificiality that excuses itself. There is a fitness and propriety in it, which, when contrasted, as it may be, with the farmer's clumps of pasture shade, his wayside trees, and his leafy screen of the farm buildings, is not without a certain charm.

Lands not Farmed.

THERE is, however, a higher grade of landscape beauty than can belong to lands tilled for their economic returns, just as there is a higher grade of man than the agricultural laborer. I propose to indicate some of the methods by which this higher beauty may be made to declare itself. First of all, in the immediate neighborhood of every country homestead, (the site and architecture being already determined on, and not, therefore, subject to present discussion,) there must be neatness and order; no tangled weedy growth, no paths half matted over: there must be abundant evidence of that presiding and watchful care without which every homestead, whether within or without, lacks its most considerable charm. If the beauty of the remoter landscape lie in its wild and unkempt condition, the contrast of extreme care at the house-side with such savagery, will be all the more engaging. And if the beauty of the outer landscapes lie merely in graceful and undulating forms, care around the doorstep will be requisite to mark definitely the outflow of the domestic wants and influences. The path I tread ten times a day should be smooth ; the patch of croquet ground should be reduced to absolute level, and any intruding tussock be shorn away from reach of the tender-footed gamesters ; but the walk along the further hill-side, where I go only after a long reach of days, may be only a tramped foot-path on the sward ; and the stretch of turf-land where the Alderneys are feeding may have its eyelets of dandelion and golden buttercups. But the care and order of which I speak should not be a finical nicety. Martinetism is odious everywhere. It must be a care that shall conceal itself—that shall be marked by the lack of everything disagreeable, and not be cognizable by traces of a recent broom or roller. The scar of a spade-cut is an unpleasant reminder of the art which is best when all traces of its mechanical devices are out of sight. Of course, there must be clippings and rollings, but they should be so deftly done, and with such watchfulness, as regards season, as to make the observer forget they had ever been used.

Again, it comes within the domain of landscape art to secure an agreeable lookout from the door and the cherished windows of the country homestead, whatever may be its situation. Accident or choice of site may, indeed, secure this beyond question; but, site being established, where views are limited or obnoxious objects fret the eye, it is surprising what may be done by judicious planting, and the re-adjustment of walls or fencing or hedging, to offer the pleasant lookout we demand, though it be bounded by a gunshot. With a reach of twenty rods before one's eye and in one's keeping, there is no possible excuse for not giving it charming objects to rest upon—objects that will not pall, but grow upon the affections of every true lover of the country.

Your neighbor's slatternly barn troubles you— plant it out; the toss of the tops of hemlocks will not be odious. A wavy bald wall irritates you; if needed as a barrier, cover it with wild vines, or flank it with hedging, or so plant your coppices on either side, in and out, that its line shall be indistinguishable. Is there a low bit of sedgy ground that can be made nothing of, for the reason that the adjoining proprietor (who holds the lower lands) will enter into none of your schemes of drainage? Plant it with rhododendrons and the red-berried alder; or if it be a mere morass, tumble into it a few of the mossy stones from the higher slopes, and equip it with the wood-ferns or clematis. There is no spot, indeed, so ungainly that it cannot be cheated of its roughness by such appliances of bush and vine and plant as our own woods will furnish; no stretch of lawn so meagre that you may not throw across it morning and afternoon, such splintered bars of light and shadow from its encompassing trees as will charm the looker-on. In all places of limited range, and which, from the necessities of position, are without wide-reaching views, it is doubtful if the eye should be allowed to rest upon any very determinate and defined barrier, as marking the extreme limit of the grounds. An irregular belt of wood or lesser growth of shrubbery will offer pleasant concealment and take away the sharpness of limitation, while some picturesque feature in a neighbor's grounds beyond, though it be only a dove-cot or the ventilator upon the barn-roof, or a gardener's cottage, may, by the vagueness and indeterminate character of the intervening barrier, become more surely yours by the possession of the eye. It is specially the province of the art we are considering, to avail itself of all within reach of the view, whatever may lie between, and make it contribute to the oneness of the home picture. True art does not inquire who made the pigments, or whose name they bear, but only, will they

8*

add to the effect of the work in hand ? If, by cutting a few trees from the copse upon the hill-side, I
can bring my neighbor's broad-armed windmill into
view, I am taking a very legitimate means of availing
myself of his expenditure ; and if the usual anchor-
age-ground for my neighbor's yacht is shut off only
by a tuft of shrubbery upon my lawn, I will cut it
away and enjoy his yacht (at anchorage) as much as
he.

There are many country places which from their
position, possess an outlook so broad and grand as
to demand no consideration of special views, and
where landscape art will find range not only in the
ordering of lesser details, but in partial concealment
of the beauties that confront the eye. The situations
to which I allude are upon such range of highland as
to offer—very likely from the adjoining public road—a
similar width of view ; but the house-view must have
some special consecration of its own—some veil of
intervening foliage may be, through which the ravish-
ing distance shall come by glimpses ; some embower-
ment of trees, under which, as in a rural framing, the
great picture of the rivers and the mountains shall
take new sightliness ; some tortuous walk through impenetrable shrubberies, from the midst of whose dim-
ness you shall suddenly burst out upon the glory of
the far landscape. Such devices are needful not only

to qualify the monotony of one unvarying scene, be-
wildering from its very extent—not only to distinguish
the home view from that of every plodder along the
highway, but furthermore, and chiefly, to show such
traces of art management as shall quicken the zest
with which the natural beauties, as successively unfolded, are enjoyed. A great scene of mountains, or
river, or sea, or plain, is indeed always a great scene;
but in the presence of it a country home is not necessarily a beautiful home. To this end, the art that
deals with landscape effect must wed the home to the
view; must drape the bride, and teach us the piquant
value of a " coy, reluctant, amorous delay."

Again, it should be a cardinal rule in landscape
art (as in all other art, I think) not to multiply means
for producing a given effect. Where one stroke of
the brush is enough, two evidence weakness, and
three incompetency. If you can secure a graceful
sweep to your approach-road by one curve, two are
an impertinence. If a clump of half a dozen trees
will effect the needed diversion of the eye and produce the desired shade, any additions are worse than
needless. If some old lichened rock upon your lawn
is grateful to the view, do not weaken the effect by
multiplying rocks. Simple effects are the purest and
best effects as well in landscape art as in moral
teaching.

A single outlying boulder will often illustrate by contrast the smoothness of a lawn better than the marks of a ponderous roller.   One or two clumps of alders along the side of a brooklet will designate its course more effectively and pleasantly than if you were to plant either bank with willows.   A single spiral tree in a coppice will be enough to bring out all the beauty of a hundred round-topped ones.   Because some simple rustic gate has a charming effect at one point of your grounds, do not for that reason repeat it in another.   Because the Virginia creeper makes a beautiful autumn show, clambering into the tops of one of your tall cedars with its five-lobed crimson leaflets, do not therefore plant it at the foot of all your cedars.   Because at some special point the red rooflet of a gateway lights up charmingly the green of your lawn, and fastens the eye of visitors, do not for that reason make all your gateways with red rooflets.   If some far-away spire of a country church comes through some forest vista to your eye, do not perplex yourself by cutting forest pathways to other spires.

Again, (and I think I have trenched upon this topic previously in the course of these pages,) every possessor and improver of a country estate, however small or however large, should work upon clearly defined plans, decided upon from the beginning.   I do not mean to say that diagrams and surveyor's maps may be positively necessary, provided the director of the improvements has a clear understanding of the boundaries and surface, and a clear understanding of the effects he wishes to accomplish. I only insist that promiscuous planting, and the laying down of paths, little by little, or year by year, without reference, clear and constant, to the final results, and to a plan that shall embrace the whole property, will involve great waste of labor, and the inevitable undoing in the future of what may be done to-day. Of course, where such work is intrusted to a corps of gardeners and laborers, complete diagrams will be necessary; and it is only where the constant personal supervision of the director, whether proprietor or other, can be counted on, that such detailed exhibit of the work in hand can be dispensed with. No general plan, such as I refer to, can be safely matured without, first, full and intimate knowledge of the ground and its environs, and, second, a clear understanding of the intentions and tastes of the proprietor under whose occupancy the plan is to reach fulfilment.

I do not at all mean to say that the laws of taste in respect to landscape art are to meet revision at the will of any chance proprietor, or that the art itself has not its elemental principles which no occupant of a country estate can safely disturb. But one landholder has a *penchant* for agriculture, and wishes to make all the available acres contribute to his taste for cattle or crops; another has a horticultural mania, and wishes the outlay to take such a shape as shall most contribute to his special pursuit; still another foresees a demand for his acres as villa sites, and desires such arrangement as shall best contribute to their conversion into some half-dozen or more of attractive homesteads; and yet another wishes such improvement as shall best develop the natural features of the place, and insure the most economic treatment of the same, without any view to future sale, or to whims, whether horticultural or agricultural.

Now it is strictly within the province of landscape art to meet either or all of these views without violation of its elemental principles. I have already intimated how far the offices of husbandman and his methods of culture may be subordinated to good landscape effect: of horticulture this is even more true. In laying out with a view to ultimate division of country property for villa sites, there are certain difficulties in the way. In a general sense, it is true that the more you make beautiful a country property, the more you make it inviting for country residences. But landscape design with a view to a single ownership and a single home establishment must needs be different from one which looks to the dispersion of the property into a dozen lesser homes. Absolute unity of plan will, in such a case, be naturally out of the question. There must be some measure of sacrifice to the contingencies reckoned upon; no sacrifice of charm, indeed, when the purpose is understood: six adjoining sites, well ordered, and planted with a view to future occupancy, may embrace a thousand beauties, but will not, of course, preserve that unity of effect which would belong to a single permanent property.

On the score of taste, a competent landscape-gardener has no need to compare notes with the proprietor of country property; but he should be put in full possession of all the economies of his plan. Does he wish a reservation for agricultural purposes, for vineyard, for orcharding, more than will be essential to his household supply? Does he count upon subsequent division of the property for building purposes? These questions should meet full discussion and the outlay be adjusted thereby. But it is unfortunately true that half the owners of country estates entertain no considerations of this kind, and, entering upon their improvements with a vague improvidence, find after a lapse of years, the bulk of them useless and inconvertible. City improvements may be undertaken without long look into the future; errors may be amended as fast as brick and mortar can be piled together; but great trees do not grow in a night, or in a year. In America, we must count upon divisions and subdivisions of property. Great ancestral estates will nowhere be long ancestral. Our republican mill grinds them sharply. Hence we lack, and must always lack that artistic dealing with country estates which can count upon oneness of proprietorship for an indefinite period of years. Better to admit this in the beginning, and let our landscape art take its form accordingly, than to weary itself with imitation of what is feudally and mercilessly old. Nothing can cheat us, indeed, of the beauty of God's trees and flowers and wood-paths. Nature is as much to the occupant of a fifty-acre holding, as to the Duke of Devonshire, or the Marquis of Buccleugh. But half a thousand acres of sylvan glade and of velvety turf cannot be maintained with us from generation to generation as the feeding ground for fallow deer; it may, however, have such keeping and embellishment as shall fit it for a score of fair homes. Better the homes with cheerfulness in them than the deer-park with want shivering beyond the walls.

City and Town Parks.

THE office of a park is wholly different from that of a village green; the same demands do not suggest the two. The city square or *plaza* is the city representative of the village common: this latter being only a rural *plaza* whereon the green-sward is a more economic and appropriate pavement than stones; the incessant traffic and wear of a metropolis do not blot the grass.

The park represents not only a demand for space and trees, but a revival and reassertion of country instincts which city associations are only too apt to infold and entomb; but, however drearily infolded, there comes some day to all denizens of cities a resurrection of those earlier rural instincts which crave growth and food—an outburst, through all the stony interstices of pavement, of the love of trees and green things. Not until a city has become so large as to deny to very many living in its interior intimate association and familiarity with the encompassing belt of country will this new need declare itself strongly. Nay, in a city, whose elevated situation, gives outlook from its open spaces upon great fields of greenness around it, such need of park land will not for a long period of years be felt.

Eventually, not only will the instinctive rural longings of the masses stimulate to this struggle to recover the lost birthright of trees and turf, but the very vanities of city growth will demand a larger airing than populous streets can supply; and the man who loves a sleek team, and indulges in its display, will vie with the workman (who wants romping place for his children) in clamor for a public park. If our vanities and our healthful tastes were always as closely yoked, we should have a better growth from the yoking.   However, it may come about— whether from the natural impulses of a crowded population to ally themselves once again with the bounteous amplitude of the fields, or whether from the artificial desire to give room and exhibition to equipages—it is undeniable that all towns of ambitious pretensions and of assured and rapid growth do, after a certain period of street packing, bestir themselves in a feverish way to secure some easy lounging-place under the trees.   Unfortunately the stir is, for the most part, at so late a day, that all available or desirable localities have been secured for other purposes.   But, whatever the alternative of cost, I cannot learn that such an enterprise, when thoroughly matured and in complete operation, has ever proved a disappointment.   I have never heard of a disposition on the part of voters to rescind any appropriation for such a purpose, and to convert a public garden or park to economic uses.   I never heard of an instance where pride did not speedily attach to the public grounds, if accessible and well cared for, and where the people of such a town did not make a boast and a glory of the endowment.

Even in countries where such far-sighted improvements are effected by the *force majeure* of an Imperial edict, popular resentments or revolutions never find their leverage in such tokens of extravagance. There are not a thousand men in Paris, rich or poor, who would make quarrel with Louis Napoleon for the millions lavished upon the Bois de Boulogne, or the appointments of the Park Monceau. But there were tens of thousands of malcontents, in Louis Philippe's time, with the fortification bill, and the inclosure for private uses, of a terrace of the garden of the Tuilleries. The people may not, indeed, have a very clear sense of their wants in the matter of a public park, but once supply them attractively and accessibly, and they feel the appositeness of the supply, and cling to it with as much obstinacy as pride.

We Americans have a way of shrinking from prospective taxation, whatever the purpose of it may be; but when once fairly saddled with it, whether for the benefit of corporations or monopolies or public improvements, we bear it with a most admirable unflinchingness. The costs of public gardens or parks, if well ordered, and not made the vehicle of private peculation, are not such as would create a remonstrance from the people of any American city; and the difficulty in the way of establishment would lie not so much in a general spirit of hostility to increased taxation, (though that spirit, as I have hinted, has a wonderful catlike watchfulness,) as in the private jealousies that must be harmonized before any large real estate improvement is practicable. I defy any benevolent gentleman, in a town of thirty thousand active, and newspaper-reading inhabitants, to propose a scheme for a public garden or park, upon a designated spot of ground, without starting an angry buzz of opposition from other equally benevolent gentlemen, who see in it only a device to bring about the rapid appreciation of property which is not their own. The quick-sightedness with which the philanthropists of one side of a smallish city will detect flaws in the philanthropy of men living on the other side of a smallish city, is indeed something marvellous. Thus it happens that some brave and honest project for park or water supply, or sewerage, will welter for years in some slough of opposing doubts, all whose obstructing slime is made up of such miserable, local jealousies as I have hinted at. The same traces of satanic influence belong, I think, to the philosophers who make up our national Congress, so that our best bits of legislation seem to come upon us by accident, when our wisest legislators are asleep, or tired, or—worse.

In the days of our present civilization and education, it is hardly to be doubted that the majority of intelligent voters in any considerable town would declare for the utility of a public park or garden; but whether their wishes can be made effective for the establishment of such a result is another question, and one which must drift into the arena of town politics—where I leave it; proposing only to discuss here some of the aims of such an endowment, some of the possibilities in that direction, the conditions of its success, and permanent usefulness to the masses.

Place for Parks.

FIRST of all, a public park should be as near as possible to the town; best of all, perhaps, if in the very centre of the town, or, as in the case of some of the old walled towns of Europe, girting it with a circle of green. I hardly think any public gardens of the world contribute more to the health and enjoyment of the adjacent population than those of Frankfort-on-the-Main, which lie all about their homes, and which are planted upon the line of the old fortifications. Even the ill-kept walks upon the ancient walls of Chester and York (in England), by their nearness to the homes of the people, and by the delightful outlook they offer, are among the most cherished promenades I know. But with us, who have no girting

walls, and rarely vacant spaces about our commercial
centres, these pleasant breathing-places must be
pushed into the outskirts of our towns. I say—rarely
vacant spaces; but while I write, there occur to me
instances of beautiful opportunities neglected, one of
which, at least, I will record. The thriving little city
of Norwich, in eastern Connecticut, is situated at the
confluence of two rivers, which form the Thames.
Along either shore of the Yantic and the Shetucket,
the houses of the town are picturesquely strewed in
patches of white and gray; but between the rivers
and the lines of houses, the land rises into a great
promontory of hill—toward the east, forming a Sal-
vator-Rosa cliff, shaggy with brush-wood and cedars—
toward the south and west, a steep declivity on which
the swiftly slanting sward-land is spotted with out-
cropping ledges; to the north a gradual slope falls
easily away to the great plains, where lie the bulk of
the suburban residences. Within twenty or thirty
years the whole upper surface of this central hillock
might have been secured for the merest bagatelle, and
would have made one of the proudest public promenades imaginable, accessible to all walkers from the
south and east, and to all equipages from the north,
and offering level plateau for drives that would have
commanded the most enchanting of views; but the
occasion has gone by; inferior houses hold their

uneasy footing on the hill-side, and a gaunt-jail, which is the very apotheosis of ugliness, crowns this picturesque height.

Another little city, that of Hartford, in the neighbor State of Connecticut, has made the most of its opportunities by converting into a charming public garden a weary waste of ground that lay between its railway station and the heart of the city. The opportunity was not large, to be sure, but it was one that needed a keen eye for its development, and the result has shown that commercial thrift may not unfrequently take its lesson with profit from the suggestions of a cultivated taste. There is many a growing town having somewhere within its borders such unsuspected aptitude and capability, that only needs an eye to discern it, and the requisite enterprise to develop in the very heart of the population a garden and a public promenade that would become a joy forever. It must be remembered, furthermore, that it is quite impossible to make such transmutation of waste and unsightly places into an attractive area of garden-land, without increasing enormously the taxable value of all surrounding property. I recall now, in one of our most thriving seaside cities, a great slough of oozy tide-mud of many acres in extent, shut off from the harbor front by a low railway embankment, showing here and there a riotous overgrowth of wild sedges, foul with heaps of garbage, uninviting in every possible way, and yet lying within stone's throw of the centre of the city. Sandy highlands, almost totally unimproved, flank it immediately upon the west—disposed there, as it would seem, for the very purpose of furnishing easy material for the filling in of the flat below. A few thousands would accomplish this, and judicious planting and outlay would in three years' time establish a charming promenade or garden in the centre of the sea-front of the town, and there is not one of the adjoining pieces of property but would be doubled in value by the operation. The neglect of such opportunities, whether due to miserable local jealousies, or, as often happens, to the short-sightedness and indifference of municipal authorities, is surely not complimentary to our civilization.

The term "near to town," in these times of horse railways, has rather a relative than positive significance. Three miles, by a fair, broad avenue, upon which well-equipped cars are making their rounds every half hour of the day, is not half so large a distance for either the laboring or the business man to compute, as a mile and a half of ill-kept, old-fashioned turnpike road.

The truth is, that citizens of sleepy towns in the interior are losing their reckoning about distances;

they have not been educated to metropolitan estimates. The Wall Street man sneers at two miles of
walk before business ; your small broker of a country
city, on the other hand, advertises for a tenement
" within half a mile of the post-office." I never see
such an advertisement but I think some Rip Van
Winkle has just waked, and that his friends should
give him a combing and nursing.

Ready accessibility is the true measure of distance
in our day, and a town park must be easily accessible
to all classes. It must be a matter in which the
humblest citizens can take pride and comfort. Those
cities which have considerable open spaces in the
shape of " common," " green," or " squares," scattered
here and there, are the last to wake to any need of a
park which shall give drives, and such sources of
diversion as belong legitimately to a public park.
The central commons and greens may do very well
in the early stages of a city's growth, but there comes
a time when the municipal edicts forbid ball-playing
and cricket, at which date there is reason to plan
some larger forage ground for our youthful sports.

And it is precisely this forage ground for the
developing muscle of Young America that the town
park should furnish. Cricket ground, base-ball
ground, and parade ground for the ambitious troops
of the municipality should be as sedulously cared for

9

as a good roadway for carriages. A skating pond would belong fitly to the requirements, and, if no river or harbor offered better space, an opportunity for boating would be wisely included. It is not supposed that a feasible spot of ground in the neighborhood of most cities can command and make good these requirements. But much more can be done than is imagined if the best available talent is secured for the work in hand. Even in our fast days, it is quite wonderful to find what a multitude of people go to sleep upon advantages which, judiciously ordered, would make them rich. There is many a river valley, in the close neighborhood of cities, covered now with rank and unprofitable grasses, over which, at small cost, might be given flow to a lake that would wash on either shore the banks of highlands, admirably fitted for drives, and already clothed with the forest growth of half a century.

Equipment of Public Gardens.

AS I have already said, it is requisite that a town park should offer a charming drive; so far charming that every townsman will feel it incumbent on him to give each stranger guest a full view of its attractions. These latter must lie, either in commanding views of the town itself and its environs, or in landscape effects which have been wrought out by skill and attention in the park itself. Neither Hyde Park nor the Bois de Boulogne offer any commanding range of view ; the delights all lie in the neatly kept roadway, the flanking lakes and parterres, the bright, green slopes of shaven turf ; at Richmond Hill or on the Pincian at Rome, on the other hand, you forget the roadway, you forget the bits of pretty turflet, you ignore the copses, you are careless of the odor of flowers, for your eye, carrying all your perceptive faculties in its reach, leaps to the fair vision of flood and field and trees, which sweep away, in sun and in shadow, to the horizon.

Undoubtedly if the surface of adjoining country will permit, it will be far less expensive to establish a park whose charm shall lie in exterior views than one whose attractions shall consist in what the professional men call (by use of an abominable word) its *gardenesque* features. Yet, with such economic purpose, it will never do to go too far in the country. It must never be forgotten with us that the men of equipages are by no means the only class who are to participate in our æsthetical progress ; the town park, to have its best uses, must not only be within easy reach by walk or by the street tramway, but it must have, too, its spaces of level ground to allure the cricket or the base-ball players. Areas should be ample enough to prevent the possible interference of these sports, (which every sensible township would do well to encourage,) with the enjoyment of a quiet drive.

While there is no need for making the wood of a public park a complete *arboretum*, I think that special care should be taken to give specimens of all the best known timber and shade trees, and that these should be definitely marked with their botanical as well as popular names, so that strollers might come to a pleasant lesson in their seasons of idleness. The particular habits of individual specimens and of forest growths might, I think, be safely and profitably noted as lending additional interest to them, and creating a sort of fellowship with the trees. Every forester knows that oaks and maples of the same species have yet idiosyncrasies of their own—one blooming a full fortnight before its neighbor, and another taking a tawny hue, while its companion is still in full array of green. In the garden of the Tuilleries there is a chestnut which enjoys the traditional repute of showing leaflets upon the twentieth of March (hence called *Vingt de Mars*), and the venerable old tree, well known to every frequenter of the garden, has come to have a character of sanctity by reason of this early welcome of the spring. In a field within sight of my own door, there is a sugar-maple which, by some fault in the planting, or some inherent defect in the tree, has made little or no growth these last six years, and which every August—a full month before the earliest of its companions—takes on a hectic flush of color, which it carries, with the buoyancy of a consumptive, all through the autumn. This accident of coloring gives an individuality and interest to the tree which distinguishes it from all its stalwart and thrifty fellows.

I do not think a town park can ever safely be mated with a trotting course; either the trotting or the park will go under. It is not intended to speak against trotting-courses, or greased pigs, or the climbing of greased poles; but the arena for these sports is not usually such a one as to entice a quiet family man to a park drive. Quiet family men are not, to be sure, very plentiful, and are not much considered nowadays; they still subsist, however, in sufficient numbers to give a stale flavor of respectability to many of our growing provincial towns, and to shape, to a certain degree, the municipal improvments. The love for fast trotters and for trotting matches is so decided an American taste that a good trotting-course will become a cherished institution in every town of a dozen or fifteen thousand inhabitants. Indeed, I think its establishment may be regarded as a kind of necessary safety-valve, through which unusual speed and the accompanying howls may be worked off safely without frightening staid old gentlemen who keep to the quiet high-roads. A good flat, a good bottom, and a good amphitheatre of seats, are about all the requisites of an approved trotting-course, and anything picturesque in the way of trees or decorative features is an impertinence. There is no fear, therefore, that the trotting taste will ever have large interference with the demand for public parks.

It is a common mistake, I think, to imagine that anything like a finical nicety in the arrangement of turf or walks or parterres is essential to the permanent and larger utilities of a town park. This, indeed, involves great cost, and diverts from larger and more important ends. A flock or two of South-Downs, confined by movable hurdles, and under charge of some custodian, who might have his rural cottage at the gate of entrance, would keep turf in very presentable condition. After this, good drainage, hard gravelled roads—subject to monthly rolling —and judiciously disposed clumps of shade, are the main things; following upon which, as the town grows in taste or ability, the parterres of flowers and the arboretum and observatory might be superadded.

But quite above and beyond our present question of treatment is the larger one of gaining, in due time, possession of available space. No town that counts

upon its thirty or forty thousand inhabitants within
the next score of years should neglect it. There can
be no loss in its becoming a large landholder within
its own territory. If the charming but costly dis-
guisements of a park cannot be ventured upon at
once, the land may at least be turned over into a
town farm, where the town's poor may be set to the
work of combing down its roughness or preparing it
by slow degrees, earning their own support, mean-
time, for the richer ends in view. The scheme is by
no means chimerical; scores of workers, through the
less active months of the year, and who are dependent
on the town for partial support, might thus be put to
remunerative labor upon the town property. A
judicious design of a park as a finality upon the land
in question might underlie, in a measure, and qualify
the regular farm labors. A well-appointed drive
might gradually uncoil itself over the hills and
through the cultivated flats, the wood crop out upon
the cliffs, and the flowers unfold in their sequestered
nooks. It seems to me that a park or garden, growing up in this way by degrees under the tutelage of
the town, not fairly throwing off its economic and
food-providing aspect until the plantations have ripened into fulness, would have a double charm. I
commend the suggestions to such boroughs as keep
their town's poor festering in some ill-ventilated alms-

house, with limited grounds, in the foulest suburb of
the place.

Burying Grounds.

EVERY considerable town requires, or will
require at no late day, not only fields for the
disport of its living swarms, but other fields (requiring exceptional care of their own) for the interment
of its throng of dead. Indeed, the living can steal
some chance moments of rural enjoyment, by bursting into fields and gardens of their neighbors, or by
plunging into untamed wilds; but a man cannot steal
a grave: there is no larceny possible to us of some
charming spot upon a neighbor's hill-side where our
bones may rest.

I cannot quite share in what seems to be the
popular disposition nowadays—to make a favorite, if
not fashionable drive of the cemetery. That it should
be beautiful, that it should carry report of the delight-
some things of every season in its flowers, its fading
wealth of leaves, its evergreens, I can well understand. But that it should be made *voyant*, inviting
chance-comers, offering views of sea or environs,
cheating one into the belief that he is in a well-kept
garden, and not among graves, lured thither by views
or prettinesses of landscape design and not by the

memories or the sentiment of the place—this is awkward. Hence, it seems to me that a sheltered hill-
side, a glen, a protected valley, are far more appropriate than a plain, scalding in the sun, or heights
which invite by a great range of exterior views.
Tastes will differ widely in this regard; but it
certainly does appear as if the whirl of lively and
clattering equipages day after day along the edges of
the graves of quiet men would make a terribly per-
turbed sleep for them; and if real grief ever stalk
thither to pay a last melancholy tribute, it must
needs make a sad public exhibition of itself, or practise a galling reticence.

In dealing with the question of a public cemetery,
adequate to the needs of a growing population—as in
the question of a public park,—our larger towns show
a provoking delay, blinding themselves year after
year to the necessities of the case, and deferring
positive action, until the needed investment assumes
gigantic proportions. There are scores of towns
whose cemeteries are absolutely brimming with the
dead, who yet take no decisive measures for an
increase of the privilege we all sigh for at last—of a
quiet sleep under trees.

Among the requisites for a country cemetery are to
be named, I think, first, a distance not exceeding forty
minutes drive from town; next, a feasible soil, and one

9*

not underlaid with ledges. An absolutely dry soil is
also desirable, and a sheltered position: for in the
last tender offices of respect to the dead, we are
exposed to all seasons, and a harsh sweep of northerly
winds adds dismally to the chill of a wintry burial.
I think we love to catch, too, in such localities, the
first warm beat of the spring sunshine, and that we
welcome the early violets on graves we know, as we
welcome them nowhere else.

If with all these requirements can be associated
picturesque variety of surface, secluded glens and
pools, where, as in Mount Auburn, water flowers
show their white regalia, it would be well; but there
should be no sacrifice of the quiet seclusion which
should belong to such a spot to compass the garish
charms of over-nice and pretentious gardening.

Park gardening and decoration is one thing; that
of cemeteries is quite another. Aims, treatment,
effects, all should be different. Sombre masses of
wood, heavy shadows, these should be present; above
all things, there should be avoidance of those sudden
surprises and graceful deceits by which gardeners
sometimes win their lesser honors. Great simplicity
of design is also essential, not only as in keeping
with the sepulchral offices of such ground, but being,
to a certain extent, proof against the harm which an
elaborate plan must suffer by injudicious planting in
private inclosures.

From the fact last named—the giving over of individual lots to private caprices of planting or arrangement, no consummate or finished gardening can, of course, ever be looked for in our cemeteries. The general effect will be at best spotty, and lack coherence. The trail of the principal drives or walks, the establishment of the capital masses of foliage, the ordering and adaptation of the encircling belt, the finish and appointments of the entrance-way—these are the objects which will demand taste and skill for their happy execution. To twirl a great labyrinth of serpentine paths through a forest, shaven clean of its under-brush—to throw rustic bridges over a flow of sluggish ditch-water, and to construct grottoes where they sit like mountebanks in the hollows of the hills, is not good gardening for cemeteries—if it be good anywhere. If there be great reach of irregular surface, there should be sunny glades to contrast with masses of solemn shade. Rustic or other littlenesses should not pique and arrest attention. The story of the place should be told in the largest letters of the gardener's vocabulary and the interpretation easy—*quiet—seclusion—REST.*

Something might be said of the character of the trees which should be planted in these fields of the dead. The willow is the traditional weeper, and in place ; but such product of the gardener's art as a

weeping ash is a terribly starched mourner, and
should be banished as an impertinence. All curious
and rare exotics, I should say, have no place there;
unless, like the yew or the European cypress, they
bear some story of association which chimes evenly
with the solemn shadows around. The darker evergreens generally, are most fitting; and there is a
variety of the Norway spruce, with long, pendulous
arms, that is one of the stateliest and comeliest and
friendliest of mourners it is possible to imagine. If
the Mediterranean cypress would but withstand the
rigor of our season, its dark plumes, leading up on
either side to the gateway of a tomb, would make a
standing funereal hymn.

Near to Savannah, in Georgia, and upon one of
the creeks making into the irregular shores thereabout, is a cemetery called, if I remember rightly,
Buena Ventura. In old times, any visitor at the Pulaski
used to find his way there, and was richly repaid for
the visit. There was no proper "keeping" to the
grounds. You passed in under a lumbering old gate-
way of unhewn timber; the paths were not carefully
tended; there was much of rampant and almost indecorous undergrowth; the tombs were mossy, and
the graves, many of them, sunken; but great live-
oaks over-reached your path, and from their gnarled
limbs hung swaying pennants of that weird gray

moss of the Southern swamp lands—festooned, tangled, streaming down—now fluttering in a light breeze, and again drooping, as if with the weight of woe, to the very earth. There was something mysteriously solemn and grave-like in it. The gnarled oaks and the slowly swaying plumes of gray told the completest possible story of the place. Had there been no tombs there, you would have said that it was the place of places where tombs should lie and the dead sleep. I have alluded to the scene only to show what and how much may be done by foliage and tree limbs, with their investing mosses, to give character to such a spot.

Neither the live oak nor the Spanish moss is available, indeed, in our Northern latitudes; but there are various degrees of fitness in the trees at command. The yew and the compact-headed Austrian pine, and the balsam fir are always in their sables; even the much-degraded Lombardy poplar, in full vigor, carries a ceremonious, self-possessed stiffness not unbefitting; while the glittering leaved beech, and hornbeam, on the contrary, with their ceaseless, idle flutter, are the most unseemly of chatter-boxes. The ash, again, without liveliness of color has great dignity of carriage, and in its half mourning of autumn purple is one of the stateliest and fittest of attendants.

I know there is a philosophy which denies the

propriety of seeking for, or multiplying any solemn symbols in connection with death, or the places where the dead lie ; which believes in opening wide and laughing landscapes around graves, and in smothering all memory of the short-lived, funeral black under the gayest of colors. It seems to me, however, that so far as such a philosophy puts its meddlesome liveliness upon church-yards and tombs, it is only a gay hypocrisy. Death is always death ; and the place where the dead lie, always Golgotha. The real grief that goes thither with its bitterness, will be put down by no pelting of bright colors, and mock grief may be mended by what solemnity belongs to the scene.

We are not to go through the world mourning, it is true ; but the graveyards, thank God, are only in scattered places. And if we can spend liveliness and cheer over all the rest of our ways, we can surely afford to leave the funereal plumes hanging over the one little path where we mourn.

V.

MR. URBAN AND A COUNTRY HOUSE.

V.

MR. URBAN AND A COUNTRY HOUSE.

Real Estate Purchase.

WHAT on earth my friend Mr. Urban wants of a farm of fifty acres, I do not know; but he wants it. At least he says as much; and I am not the man to dispute him. I feel assured that when he gets it, he will grow red in the face over it, and perspire fearfully, and use language forbidden in the decalogue, and find his pet Alderneys, season after season, very obstinately dropping calves of the wrong sex, and his steers breaking into his cabbage patch. I am confident that he will feel persuaded, before the end of the first year, that all his country neighbors have conspired to fleece him, and that the butchers are all cut-throats—in which opinion he will not

be far out of the way. Notwithstanding this, which
I have represented to him in the mildest manner possible, (seeing his infatuation,) Mr. Urban still wants
a fifty-acre farm. Of course, he is no farmer; and his
idea of a good farmer is of one who raises large vegetables, keeps his fences and buildings in Pimlico
order, and owns fine stock. It is, I must be allowed
to say, a somewhat imperfect idea. He has not the
slightest doubt of his capacity to treat land judiciously, and make it produce huge crops at a minimum cost. How he expects to accomplish this, I
do not know; neither, I think, does he.

Naturally, he does not mean to buy a farm full
of rocks; on the contrary, he wishes smooth land—
rich, of course, with no uncouth assemblages of
brush—gently undulating withal—giving fine views
—not hard to till, with serviceable buildings upon
it—in a healthy region, convenient to schools, railways, churches, mills, steamboats, and the world
generally—with ample society in the neighborhood
—plenty of the choicest fruit—abounding in good
spring-water—no incumbrances, and at a very low
price. All this, he thinks, is to be found easily, any
day in the week, and that a moderate sized check
will transfer it to his possession.

There is a little presumption in the thought;
but, if the advertisements are to be believed, not

much. City-bred men have indeed rather a presumptuous way of regarding those who live and gain their living by country pursuits.

Think of it for a moment :—Here (in the country) is your quiet landholder, living in the performance of a humble range of duties—rearing brown-cheeked boys, who will make their way to high places of trust—to generalships, to governorships, by dint of their sturdy habits of self-denial, and of work, which have belonged to their early life ; and, on the other hand, yonder by the gas-lights is your business man of the city, rearing boys under the shadow of the Broadway shops, who, by reason of no self-denial at all, will hardly arrive at the governing even of themselves (to say nothing of States) ; and yet, such a person counts it no difficult matter, by the gains of only a week's profitable venture, to oust the countryman from his home, and take possession of his lands. It is lamentable to think that the accomplishment of such undertaking is so easy. An instinctive clinging to one's home, is a good nucleus for the growth of orderly virtues. I am not going to enter into the question as to whether the better man may grow up under trees, or under brick walls; it is a large question ; and there is a leafy side to it, which, to me, is particularly engaging : but to-day, our concern is with Mr. Urban and his search and its results.

As I have said, the advertisements are most promising—so also are the representations of the real estate agents, (the most citified of citizens,) who are loudest in their praises to a new comer—of some property, dull of sale, which has been a long time on their books.

And here, I wish to interpose, by way of parenthesis, a suggestion—our need of a more intelligent and trustful real estate agency (so far as relates to country homes,) than now exists. It should be in the hands of parties who have lived in the country, who are familiar with the country, and with country resources, and country drawbacks, who by travel and experience are competent to advise, and who by large intercourse with landholders can put an inquirer on the right trail. Still further, it is eminently desirable that such party be able to furnish leading hints for whatever changes may be requisite —the system of management that may be safely pursued, and to forecast the home which is sought for. I am by no means suggesting what is impracticable, or impossible. Older countries have long seen the advantages of such agency as I describe. A man of business in London, who after a series of successes conceives the idea of establishing a country home, is able to put himself at once in communication with certain well-known parties, who (though they may

not advertise in the journals,) are understood to be
in correspondence with such landholders as are willing to sell, but entertain a horror of seeing their
homes and lands trampled over day after day by
whatever curious people may obtain a search ticket
from the established and ordinary real estate agents.
A home is a home, even to the humblest; and to
those whose needs demand a peremptory sale, the
interposition of some adroit agent who makes the
visit of a purchaser appear to be only the visit of a
curious friend, is an immense relief.

Still more important is it that such negotiator be
competent to give advice based upon long experience
and observation. There is many a man, my friend
Urban among them, who, conceiving a longing for
the quietude or other indulgences of the country, has
yet the most dim and vague notions of what he is
really in search of. Is it simply a quiet reach of
garden ground which may supply all the enjoyment
of the lesser fruits? Is it sea air alone—or mountain
air, simply—without a thought or care of anything
beyond? Is it shade and trees, and a taste of wild-
ness? Is it the care of fine cattle and the requisite
attention and expenditure? Is it a two months'
disport with a model-farm in summer, without much
regard to the returns? Is it the establishment of a
country home which shall be complete in all its equip-

ments ?   Not one in ten of those freshly smitten with
a desire to purchase a country residence can definitely
say.   So much the more need of one who can intelli-
gently, by a few practical questions, interpret their
own wishes to the purchasers themselves and fathom
the full reach of their country longings.

Cost and Returns of Fifty Acres.

A FARM of fifty acres may be a large thing, or it
may be a small thing ; small, if remote, and
submitted only to the " hand to mouth " culture of a
great many of the present holders ; but large, extrav-
agantly, if it be favorably placed, and be wrought to
the full measure of its capacity by the best appliances
of agricultural and horticultural art.   Yet the applicant at the city offices can form no idea of this distinction, nor will his queries in such a quarter put
him in the way of arriving at the just grounds of such
distinction.   If, on the other hand, such applicant
(Mr. Urban, we will say,) were to address himself to
one of wide experience and observation in such
matters, he would probably say : " My dear sir, do
you wish a fifty acre farm, that shall return revenue ?
Do you wish it as a plaything, for which you will be
willing to pay as much annually as for your opera-box
and its attendant expenses ?   Do you wish to engage

your sympathies in the affair, and demonstrate some improved method of culture at whatever cost? Finally, do you wish it as a summer home, enjoyable —through all the time of leaves and fruitage—and not a cancer upon the purse through all the remaining months of the year?"

Well—not one in ten who talks vaguely about having a farm—a country place—is prepared to answer intelligibly and directly such questions. Can you—who have sometimes thought of giving your children breathing-room, under trees? Can you— who have sometimes thought of glorifying your business successes in Wall Street, by a tasteful home in the country? Can you—publisher, jobber, grocer, bookseller, tailor—who have some vague notions of eventually giving dignity to your gains by establishing a home under elms—have you any precise idea of what you propose? What limit of land—what range of landscape—what fertility of soil—what addenda of convenience?

I don't think, for a moment, that you have; I don't think that one in a hundred has, who amuses himself in dreamy hours with forecasts of a pleasant home in the shade of oaks, and in the midst of corn-lands, which, in boyish days, he knew—only too well. The man who is eager for a town purchase of house or lot, has very distinct notions (ordinarily) of the

size he covets—the number of rooms requisite—of
the household service he will possibly require, and
of the probable range of his annual costs in maintaining the same. But, with respect to the country,
whenever his aspirations turn in that direction, he is
in a maze. He counts it an indulgence, which, like
city indulgences, has no determined laws of cost ; it
is another opera-box, of which the trees make the
upholstery, and some Killarney manager presents the
bills in brogue. Under these conditions of uncertainty, an intermediate agent, who can interpret in
some measure a man's own indefinite wishes, and by
a few direct, practical questions, reduce his intentions
to form, is eminently needed—one, moreover, who,
by his own experience and observation, can suggest
the costs and capabilities of farm, garden, or country
seat, and enable the purchaser to take a complete
trade view of his proposed enterprise.

To return to Mr. Urban—his negotiations must
be largely through the established real-estate offices,
or by personal reply to the newspaper advertisements. These leave him in a dreary muddle. Those
who have had experience, know why, and how. The
established agencies take no account of an applicant's
tastes, or positive wants, (if he were able intelligibly
to express them,) and are only anxious to make sale ;
the advertisements are naturally exaggerated to a

degree that makes the consequent search a ludicrous bore. One "charming place" is next to a great reach of marsh land, where every informant is pale and quaking with the ague; another is so beset with rocks that it would require double the cost of purchase to clear a smooth bit of greensward at the door.

Such incongruities naturally shock a man of commercial susceptibilities—if he proposes to carry them to the country with him. Mr. Urban does; and, fretted by an accumulation of mischances, and of misdirections, as well as by not a little conscious ignorance of his own, appeals to me for certain practical hints in way of guidance—putting his appeal indeed in the shape of a rambling talk, which I take the liberty of digesting into this formulary of questions :—

1st. How much ought fifty acres of land, with respectable farm-house, and out-buildings, within accessible distance—say not over three to four hours from the city—to cost?

2d. Will the possible or probable revenue from such a farm be sufficient to keep it in good order—best of order, say—so that it shall not become a bill of expense?

3d. What crops or treatment will insure such return, without destroying altogether the picturesque

10

effects, or requiring me to cut every tree upon the place?

4th. Is it possible to secure any decent man, without too big a raft of children, to supervise such a farm—live in the back rooms—keep the smell of his cabbage stews sufficiently under cover, so as to enable me to enjoy a country home in-doors—(when I wish) and relieve me of all the fatigue of details?

5th. Supposing I purchase such a place, and stock it to my fancy, and reorganize the old house, or possibly, build a new one, and Mrs. Urban grows tired of it all, in a year, or two, or three, is there any hope of my getting back my purchase money and costs, or a sum ranging within fifty per cent. of the same?

6th. What are the best cattle to keep, (supposing I purchase,) and are any pears better upon the whole than the Bartletts, and do you know of a maid of all work, who would milk upon a pinch, and stay away from mass for a fortnight; and is the patent churn, on show at the corner of Broadway and Cedar street, really a good article?

7th. Which do you think the best for eggs, the Brahma Poutras, or the Cochin Chinas, and do they require much care?

8th. What do you think of Jersey for a country residence?

When a man's rambling conversation for two or three hours is capable of digest into such interrogative formulæ, it is evident that he has some rural intentions; and I proceed to reply to such (in behalf of my friend Urban) seriously and *seriatim*.

The price of land, within the required distance of New York, is as variable as the weather. There are lands within a radius of a hundred miles of the City Hall, equipped with rocks and trees, which would be dear at ten dollars the acre, and there are lands within the same radius, equipped with rocks and trees, and without architectural improvements, which would be cheap at two thousand dollars per acre. In fact, there is no rule for price of land, as prices rule for other commodities. Lands along the Hudson, for instance, are valued—for their river views, or, may be, the social attractions of their neighborhood—at prices upon which the best ordered cropping would not pay a rental of one per cent. On the other hand, there are level garden grounds on Long Island to be bought at prices on which eight, ten, and even fifteen per cent. might be made secure by judicious culture. Within four miles of Edinboro Castle there are grass-lands which rent, per acre, for one hundred and fifty dollars a year. Of course, near to great cities, the rental of gardening or grazing-land, is measured by the length of lease—if long, it is worth more; if ·

short, it is worth less. In general, I should say that any easily-tilled, fairly productive land, within three miles of a good market, (by which I mean any city of twenty-five to forty thousand inhabitants,) ought, upon a ten years' lease, to pay a rental of at least twelve to fifteen dollars per acre. This supposes, however, full agricultural or horticultural aptitude on the part of the manager—a qualification which rarely belongs to city purchasers. If such a purchaser looks simply to agricultural rental, as a justification of the enterprise, he can hardly afford to pay more than two hundred or two hundred and fifty dollars an acre for lands adapted to easy tillage. But a largely qualifying circumstance lies in the fact that all such lands near to centres of business, take on annual increase of value by reason of the growth of the town. In the last ten years such rate of increase in all thriving neighborhoods might safely be reckoned at six to eight per cent. for each twelvemonth. This is, however, only true of those farm-lands which lie so near to cities or large towns, as to suggest the outlay of new roads across them, or a prospective demand for suburban building lots. In view of this, the sagacious purchaser of a fifty acre farm will not leave out of view—if he desires the surest possible increase of his capital—the attractiveness of the land for building sites ; and if, as we suppose, his purchase be within fifteen to twenty minutes' drive of a growing city, he will project his improvements, whether of planting or grading, with an eye to its ultimate adaptation for such purpose.

Will the farm revenue of fifty acres pay for care and keeping? Most unquestionably, if there be a reasonable amount of smooth tillable land, and average fertility, and no woful mismanagement. If, however, "care and keeping" are understood to imply the introduction of gravelled walks in all directions, and trenching for shrubbery, agricultural returns will scarcely pay for the weeding and the watering. Luxuries are luxuries all the world over, and must be paid for out of hand. What I count legitimate care and keeping, is such management as shall insure a gradually cumulative fertility to the cultivated portions, a neat and orderly air to the necessary buildings and walks, and a gradual but positive development of those features which contribute most to its attractiveness as a place of residence.

As for the proceeds of a sudden sale growing out of disgust with the rural enterprise, I should hope that a man—or a woman either—might be duly punished for such vacillation of purpose. 'Twould be a good ethical result, whatever might be its economies to the Urban adventurers. Any such quick-coming disgust arises, I think, in the majority of instances, from the lay out of more considerable improvements than can be thoroughly kept in hand or matured : and it is needless to say that no new purchaser will ever pay a large price for gravel walks overgrown with turf, or gullied by the rains, or for shrubbery that leads a starveling life in a great encompassing circle of foul growth. An inferior plan completed is always more salable than a grandiose scheme but half carried out. Again, ornamental country architecture never brings its cost, save under very exceptional conditions; therefore the proprietor who forecasts a possible early sale, should be very coy of placing much capital in flamboyant joinery or expensive walks.

On the other hand, whatever expenditure contributes to the real productive capacity of the land, whether in the way of drainage, or permanent fertilizers, or judicious farm buildings proper, will prompt buyers, and in nine cases in ten, return its full cost. The man who spends five thousand dollars in bringing up the revenue of a fifty-acre farm from four hundred to a thousand dollars a year, is working upon a safe basis; but the man who expends an equal sum in finical equipments of house and garden, and in the shaping of a great mass of walks and the planting of exotics—while the land remains

at its old fixed point of productiveness—*may* find
buyers who will refund the cost of his whims; but
the chances are by no means in his favor.

Another large source of disgust with rural under-
takings lies in the difficulty of finding efficient and
honest directing labor. We have in this country no
class of farm bailiffs who, by education and tradition,
know their duties, and quietly perform them. We
have indeed shipments, from year to year, of stray
specimens of this old country class; but the demo-
cratic instinct speedily overtakes them—of becoming
directors in chief. As good democrats—which of
course all Americans are—we ought not to regret
this, but it comes awkwardly in the way of a great
many city visions of rural felicitude. Mike, who has
toiled far into the twilight, under the shadows of the
hills of Wicklow, comes deftly and easily into a ten-
hour system, by virtue of which, on some June day
your out-spread hay lies smoking under the evening
dew; and Bridget, the stout lass, red-armed, and
crimson-checked, commended for all work, who has
milked the spotted kine in the folds that border
Killarney, "many a time, and oft," is quick to com-
prehend the American deference for the sex, and
explodes upon you with "Shure! and it's niver a
woman's work!"

But, short-comings of subordinates could be borne,

if we might be sure of the intelligent and faithful direction of superiors. In fault of this from outside sources, Mr. Urban, if he insists upon his fifty-acre experiment, must undertake it himself. And, in that event—as I hinted at the beginning—I expect to see him grow fearfully red in the face, and struggle against his wife's repinings, and yet, through all—if the rural love be strong in him—work out results that will be charming in spite of their toils.

As for the pears and the Chittagongs, about which, if I remember rightly, my friend Urban instituted some inquiries, I have nothing in particular to say. Bad fruit is due more to lack of good culture, than to choice of bad varieties; let a man select the best specimens he can find in the city-markets—testing them by taste—secure the trees from a nurseryman who has a reputation to lose, then cultivate with care, and he will never lack good fruit.

There is as much dilettanteism in pomology as in old pottery, or in poetry; a sound man who wearies of the dilettanti chooses what he likes, and gives it protection and reaps his reward. I would as soon think of choosing my fruits by the advices of the horticultural disputants, as of choosing my pictures (if I ever bought them) by the advices of the newspaper critics. The pomologists stand related to those who raise fruit for home enjoyment, and under fair garden culture, as the lexicographers and philologists are related to those who use language to enwrap a sermon or a plea; a finical nicety, if it engross them, will be at the cost of vigor and directness of thought.

So of the improved races of poultry. The hen-fanciers are, I dare say, very worthy people; far be it from me to pluck a feather from the tail of any of their brood. But to my obscure sense, an egg is always very much of an egg, whatever fowl may have the laying of it. Nor can I detect much difference between a " broiler " of the Chittagong, or any other heathen family, and the " broiler " Bridget may dress, and lay before me at a June breakfast, from the cackling company that have always laid and scratched about the dung-hills of our Christian country. Nay, I take a rather pleasant entertainment in fancying my cheerful and cackling barn-door brood are lineally descended from those veterans of the British roost, who, under the name of Chanticleer, have for so many centuries lifted up their welcome to the morn-ing. There are family associations which are a source of pride; what if my gallant fellow in white, yonder, with golden legs, and blood-red comb, curveting with wings down-spread, and giving a coquettish look to the demure feathered people of his harem, comes in direct lineage from the alert old Chanticleer of the House that Jack Built ?

10*

This is the cock that crowed in the morn,
That waked the priest all shaven and shorn,
That married the man all tattered and torn, etc.

Can we say as much, or fancy as much for an
awkward, frizzled creature of Shanghae name, as
stupid as the celestials with their hair tied into a
cue?

And yet those city gentlemen who have come
newly into possession of fifty acres, or ten acres of
farm land, are prone to distress themselves with the
notion that they have not precisely the right breed
of cattle, or hens, or geese. Their griefs (allow me
to say)—for they will have them—will not rest upon
so inconsiderable a base as a wrong choice of animals;
any of God's creatures will be good enough, if they
give them requisite care.

Question of Localities.

I PERCEIVE even now that I have not replied
to every query of my friend Urban. "What do
I think of New Jersey as a residence?"

I know a great many excellent people in New
Jersey—entirely unconnected with its railway system.
I have reason to believe that there are villages in the
retired parts of the State where the houses and door-

yards are neat, and where the streets are not filled with offal and mangy dogs. Fifty acres of land in New Jersey—soil being equal—will bear as good corn or rye as in any other spot of our common country where the sun shines with equal force. I do not indeed think that "Vineland" is soon to become our Eden, or that, if we ever have an Eden, it will lie in New Jersey. If a Euphrates were ever to spring up in the Highlands, I doubt much if it could ever cross the Central or the Camden and Amboy track—without good lobby management. All this, however, is said jokingly.

There are good farms in New Jersey; there is most excellent garden-ground, and—best of all—one can come from it easily to New York. There is no reason why its near lands should not become the paradise of fruiterers, and of vegetable-growers for the market. Its general surface—short of the mountains, or of the beautiful rolling lands of Monmouth—does not invite those who look for the picturesque as well as the practical.

But what boots it, talking of this or that locality? If a man has really made up his mind to be shaven, it matters little on which half of his chin the operator shall commence. If Mr. Urban, or any other good friend, is determined to possess himself of fifty acres, he will undoubtedly have associations which will draw him in this or that direction, against all reasoning upon the mere merit of the land.

Agriculturally speaking, it does not much matter where the amateur farmer may go. I do not say this ironically, but in full soberness. If a man, used to city life and its lusts, has made up his mind to redeem himself, so far as he may, by grappling with fifty of God's acres, and by putting the stamp of his energy and toil upon them, he cannot go wrong, wherever, within reasonable distance, the hills and the meadows are spread out. Earnest work will declare itself effectively, on the harsh rocky banks of the Hudson, or upon the unctuous level of Jersey. This much, however, is to be said practically—the nearer a man can establish himself to one of those great avenues of travel—that is, toward Philadelphia, Boston, or Albany—the more sure he will be of finding sale in the event of failure, and the more sure of ready and constant market for whatever produce he may have on hand.

I am perfectly well aware that my friend Mr. Urban (and others of like humor) will insist that he has no intention of selling out or of marketing extensively. It is pleasant, however, to feel that we can do such things if we choose. From my own observation I am persuaded that the man who has no chance of selling his country place or his farm is always a great deal more eager to sell than the one who has opportunities flowing upon him weekly. Above all things, it is imperative that a proprietor who would enjoy to the full a delightful country place, or a well-managed farm, should allow others to enjoy it with him. By which I mean, that his improvements and successes should be in the sight of people, and not in some utterly inaccessible locality, out of view and out of mind.

To plant charming shrubberies and lay down captivating walks in quarters that no one can reach but by a break-neck scramble over abominable roads, is like making a fine speech to empty benches—always an ungrateful thing to do, as many a good man knows. Half the charm of the river-bank places along the Hudson lies in the fact that they, with their surroundings, really form a part of that great water highway of travel—gazed upon every summer day by the world that floats downward and upward through the mountain gates of the river, dotting the green hills with lessons which every floating traveller may read—massing their showy rhododendrons so that thousands from below and above may see the pink crown of blossoms. The boat, the car, those hundred eyes, do not steal away any home-like privacy; they equip it rather with a new content—the content that comes of seeing others enjoy what we

enjoy and take a pride in ourselves. Never a man
yet, no matter how crotchety or unassailable, who
possessed farm or garden, into whose management
his pride and care had largely entered, but enjoyed
seeing it admired. The eye of the world upon a
man's work is healthfully stimulative. He who
denies it, and plants for his solitary gratification only,
has a weak spot in his head or heart, and deserves to
go crazed in an island-garden. There are charming
places, so far as banks and trees and water view go,
along the far away shores of Long Island, but it is a
long day's journey to reach them over a road where
nobody travels. There are very grateful, inaccessible
nooks in Rockland County, where

" A hermit hoar, in solemn cell,"

might wear out life's " evening gray," very jollily;
but no man who wants his flowers to catch a new
tint from the reflected grace of fair faces, wishes to
bury himself there. There are magnificent grazing
farms in the wilds of Greene County, great waves of
rolling hills, great Tors of shaggy, shaded cliff, great
wealth of brooks, purling amid the undulations of the
meadows, great rampant crests of forest growth, with
century-old hemlocks piling out of them their wondrous pagodas of green ; but who wants the torture
of a drive over the Catskills to enjoy it all ?

Mr. Urban does not, neither do I.

Testimony of Experts.

A T the risk of iteration, and in the hope of throwing all possible light upon the subject under
notice, I propose the examination of a few fifty-acre
farmers, who shall represent respectively the stock-
breeder, the amateur, the business man, the philosopher, the practical man and the trader.

Mr. Urban being in company—in whose interest
the inquiries are made—we first encounter Mr. Upden, of Deep-Dale, well known among Committee
men, and eminent at Agricultural Fairs.

His system is simply—to breed cattle of pure
blood. We venture the query—if Mr. Upden's stock
is fed mostly from the land, or if he is in the habit
of buying food?

Witness. "I buy, I should say, from twenty to
forty tons a year."

Mr. Urban innocently asks if Mr. Upden makes
sufficient butter for the consumption of his family?

The question is almost resented.

"Butter-making is an annoyance. Six or seven
hundred dollar cows can be put to better uses. I
prefer to buy my butter."

Query. "We are to suppose then, I think, that

the milk of your cows goes to the rearing of your young animals.   Does this prove sufficient?"

Witness. "In most instances; we sometimes, however, purchase native animals to suckle our choice calves."

Query. "With the milk from two cows, I suppose, you are able to rear a fine calf?"

Witness. "That is our intention."

Query. "Is it your opinion that a calf so reared will be able to sustain itself in good condition without extra feeding for a series of years?"

Witness. "I do not understand the term 'extra feeding.' It is our way to give animals whatever they will eat at whatever cost."

Query. "Is there an active demand for your cattle from practical farmers?"

Witness. "Not so large as we could wish. We sell mostly to breeders."

Query. "Are the prices you receive remunerative?"

Witness. "We endeavor to make them so; though with a large stock on hand we are compelled to pass off some animals on private terms."

Query. "Have the results been such as to warrant you in recommending to a friend a similar course of agricultural operations?"

Witness. "If the friend had large capital, and an

assured income, independent of his land, and had a taste for fine cattle I think I could do so."

All which is eminently discreet : but if to a taste for fine cattle, any rurally inclined gentleman adds a thorough knowledge of them, and aptitude in the handling of them, and a keen eye for the apprehension of their good or bad points, (such as few men are born to,) he may become a successful breeder. But to undertake such a business with only the flimsy basis of a love for fine cattle, will prove a very profitless venture.

The next witness is a stout man, partially bald, who carries a bandana pocket-handkerchief and perspires freely—John Heaviside, of Three-Hills Farm : retired from business going on five years.

Query. "Would Mr. Heaviside be good enough to detail in brief his system with respect to stock and labor ? "

Witness. "Well upon my word, there's not much of a system. I keep a pair of carriage-horses, and a little roadster for the boys, and a pair of mules, and a pony and a saddle-horse, and we sometimes hire a neighbor's oxen. Then there's a cow or two and their calves; and there's a foreman, and gardener, and coachman, and five out-door hands in the summer."

Query. "What are your crops principally, Mr. Heaviside ? "

Mr. Heaviside dabs the top of his head reflectively, and replies: "Grass and vegetables, I should say, mostly; and fruit—we've plenty of fruit."

Query. "Do the sales meet the expenses of the place?"

The witness gives over for a moment his exercise with the bandana and stares blankly at the questioner.

Query. "You sometimes make sales?"

Witness. "Oh! yes—four hundred quarts of blackberries, for instance, the last season. Upon my word and honor it's true."

Query. "Anything further?"

Witness. "Not that I know of. Mrs. Heaviside could tell better. She claims the sales for pin-money."

Query. "What would you reckon the probable cost of maintaining a farm of fifty acres?"

Witness. "I should put it at four thousand a year—taking one year with another."

Query. "Have you much shrubbery, and have you laid down gravel walks?"

Witness. (Dabbing cheeks and head with his bandana.) "Ouf! miles!"

Mr. Heaviside, upon being interrogated on that point, testifies that there is no lack of vegetables; indeed, he is of opinion that enough are grown for ten families; why so many he is unable to say; he believes the garden was laid out with a view to such an amount, and of course, it is necessary to keep the garden planted.

On being asked if he could suggest any more economic method of management than that at present pursued he seems at first at a loss; but being pressed for an answer " would allow forty acres of the land to grow up to wood, and drop the gravel-walks."

In the event of putting his farm on the market, could the witness hope to secure the original price with the sum for improvements added?

The witness has his doubts.

" Could he realize the original sum, with half the cost of improvements added? "

(His farm is within a half-mile of a very lovely and stagnant little town of Berkshire County.) Mr. Heaviside loses his temper and retires, being joined by a young lady in large hoops, who cheers him with the sight of a lovely new carnation, and a charming little assemblage of the new *Mathiola Bicornis.*

The next informant is Mr. Limbold, a lithe, wiry gentleman of great self-possession, and a refreshing breeziness of manner.

He has purchased a farm of fifty acres within three hours of New York; he spends three months there in mid-summer; his wife prefers Newport, but yields to him in consideration of a fortnight at the close of the season at the Ocean House. He has not built—not he ; he has added a wing sufficient for his summer accommodation. He has not employed a Scotch gardener—not he. The old owner, a practical farmer, remains in charge under agreement to share sales, the owner furnishing half stock and equipments. He transports his household the twentieth of June ; and by contract, shares the farmer's larder, adding such private delicacies as he chooses. He secures all his winter butter and poultry, and makes sales of the excess, on partnership account, to well-known dealers. The farm is not a moth to him—by no means. Returns fully balance the interest account ; and the farm, lying within three miles of a thriving city, is rapidly appreciating in value. In view of this fact, he expends five hundred a year in such improvements as will make the land more desirable for suburban sites, and in five years hence is confident of quadrupling his money.

Mr. Urban, who has wavered under the Heaviside story, is as cheerfully intent upon his farm as ever.

The next witness is a philosopher and reformer. He believes in drainage—deep drainage—in sub-soiling, in phosphates, in science, in anything almost which is told him seriously. The consequence is, he has bought a farm that no one else would buy, and has put contrabands and refugees of various sorts at work upon it, until he has expended more money to the acre than was ever expended for agricultural purposes in Orange County before.

Mr. Creed is asked at what depth he is accustomed to plant his drains?

Witness. "Four to five feet; six feet I think is better."

Query. "And if you come upon rocks?"

Witness. "I blast them out."

Query. "And you find a profit in this?"

Witness. "It's thorough."

Mr. Creed has possibly misapprehended the question.

Witness. (Sharply.) "Not at all. I can't tell about profits; we hear too much of profits; thoroughness is better. Farmers ought to do things thoroughly. I try to show them how."

"May we ask," resumes Mr. Urban, "what are your principal crops, Mr. Creed—those on which you place your main reliance?"

Witness. "I am trying at present some experiments with vetches, and a new pumpkin, recommended very strongly by Dr. Newton, of the Agricultural Department. I am also making trial of a few new grapes. I have still some faith in the Dioscorea Batata."

Query. " Would Mr. Creed recommend to an enterprising young man, or to a middle-aged man, anxious to secure a home, the purchase of a fifty-acre farm, and thorough drainage of the same ? "

Witness. " I would recommend to an honest young man to keep as clear as possible of the cities ; country gains are honest if they are small ; city gains are devilish."

Query. " Are we to understand, Mr. Creed, that the means which you have lavished upon your farm operations are derived from the land ? "

Witness. " I shall be happy, gentlemen, to further your agricultural investigations ; if you confine your inquiries to that class of subjects, I shall be glad to make reply."

Query. " Is it your opinion, Mr. Creed, that a man of energy and industry, who should purchase a farm in a retired district, and carry out your system of thorough drainage and blasting, would lay the base of permanent pecuniary success ? "

Witness. " I care very little about pecuniary success. We hear altogether too much of it. I think a young man of industry and good habits might secure a competence by hard work anywhere in the country ; and with a competency any man ought to be content. I am inclined to think that I should recommend land with as few permanent rocks as possible."

Mr. Creed, it appears further, is the owner of quite a number of pure-bred animals ; but his fences falling into a bad condition in the course of his improvements and experiments, (some of these being in the shape of patent hurdles,) and his neighbor's male animals being intrusive and aggressive, he is not quite sure of his calves. His sales, therefore, have been subject to the discount of the uncertainty, and have brought only fair butcher's prices. It is hinted that the adjoining farmers laugh at Mr. Creed's operations. But in what age have the rustics failed to laugh at a philosopher ?

We next encounter—in the person of Mr. Sloman —an eminently respectable man, of the upper part of Westchester County, who has managed his farm of fifty acres for the past thirty years.

Query. " Do you find a profit in farming Mr. Sloman ? "

Witness. " Waäl, that's as folks count profit. These 'ere chaps that go into heavy wallin' and drainin' may be don't count profit as we count it. If I keep my family along, and buildins in repair, and put up five or six hundred dollars, I call it a pooty clean thing."

Query. " Would you tell us, Mr. Sloman, something of your method ? "

Witness. " Waäl, there an't much method to

speak of. We keep ten or twelve cows through the summer, accordin' to the season; if hay is lookin' up, 'long in the fall, we fat an old cow or two, and may be a pair of cattle. We mean to keep our mowin' up and put eight or ten acres—'cordin' to the season —in corn and potatoes."

Query. "Potatoes are a pretty good crop, are they not, Mr. Sloman?"

Witness. "There an't no better crop, if a man is nigh enough to market to send in a hundred bushels a day without worryin' his team."

Mr. Sloman being asked his opinion in regard to the improved systems of husbandry, replies:

"Waäl, I've pooty much made up my mind that books is books, and farmin' is farmin'. I've nothin' to say agin these gentlemen that like to spend money a' ditchin'; I've nothin' to say agin a good tidy erittur, and you may call her Durham, or you may call her what you like. If she fills a pail she comes up to my idee of a good critter; if she doan't—she doan't. That's my opinion. May be I'm wrong; but that's my way o' lookin' at it."

An effort is made to bring back the inquiry to a more definite issue by asking Mr. Sloman "what he thinks about the labor question?"

Witness. "Waäl, good help is ruther skerce."

Your intensely practical man under question—

unused to formal investigation—is apt to bring forward the awkward facts that confront him every day, without measuring their relations. It appears in the end that Mr. Sloman pays out some four to five hundred dollars a year for labor—in addition to his own and that of his boy of fifteen. Reckoning this at five to six hundred more, it would appear that the needed labor upon a farm of fifty acres under ordinary cultivation would be not far from a thousand dollars. Meeting this, and the taxes, and " putting by " some four or five hundred from his returns, the country proprietor thinks he is doing a very fair thing. When a man of this stamp is confronted with such statements as appear from sanguine Western vineyardists, about a return of six thousand dollars per acre for land in vines, "prepared with the plow at a cost of twenty-five dollars the acre," he simply puts a fresh quid in his cheek, and indulges in remarks not creditable to the veracity of the vineyardist.

I am inclined to think that the real truth lies midway between the parties. Mr. Sloman, with his old-fashioned habits, is not accomplishing the half that ought to be accomplished with his fifty-acre farm ; the not unfrequent extraordinary representations of vineyard product, on the other hand, I cannot but regard as palpable exaggerations. I have not the

11

slightest notion that a vineyard in Missouri—however exquisite the vintage—will return the treble per acre of the Lafitte estate of Medoc. There have been exceptionable periods—as in the days of the morus multicaulis fever—when an acre under ordinary cultivation would yield its three or four thousand dollars of profit; but whoever makes such exceptional returns, whether due to wine or mulberry delirium, the basis of certain and continued horticultural successes, is either blinded by his enthusiasm, or wantonly misleads.

I record one other fifty-acre experience. Mr. Stimpson, an active, red-bearded, prompt man, is understood to have purchased some eight years since, a farm of some forty to fifty acres, within a couple of miles of the thriving city of ——, for the sum of twenty thousand dollars. Does he recommend a similar purchase to such inquirers as Mr. Urban?

Witness. "If Mr. Urban can make as good a purchase—unhesitatingly."

Mr. Stimpson has found his farming profitable then?

The witness begs to correct a possible misapprehension; his farming was not profitable. He had undertaken the raising of vegetables; but he could never find a grocer or vegetable dealer who would pay him half price for them; he undertook the small fruits, but between the destruction of baskets, small prices, or the payment of vagabond berry-pickers from the town, (who trampled down more in value than they gathered,) he abandoned that scheme ; he thinks he never bought a cow, but he paid one third more than she was worth, to the shrewd neighbors who hemmed him in ; if labor was twenty dollars a month, he could never get it under twenty-five ; his breeding sows inevitably devoured the half of their litters, though his watchfulness was constant—(perhaps too constant.) As for horses, he never bargains for one now, but he insists that he should have a spavin or two and the heaves, and by strict insistance on this, he has the satisfaction of knowing some of the defects in advance—a satisfaction he never had until he adopted the rule ; he had undertaken the sale of milk in a weak moment of resolve, but he found he was selling large quarts, whereas his rivals in the traffic were all selling small quarts—he was selling pure milk, and the neighbors were cooling down their overheated cans with an infusion of cool spring water.

In short, Mr. Stimpson declares that between discontented and overpaid laborers he could not realize four per cent. upon his purchase, with his own supervision and anxieties, (which were immense,) thrown into the bargain.

" And yet you would purchase ? "

"This is the explanation," says the witness; "the increase of population and manufactures, has brought the skirts of the town upon me. I have opened a new street or two; I have already sold three very charming sites at prices which cover all my original payment, and I have some half-dozen in hand, after the sale of which I shall still have my homestead with some four or five acres, which I can afford to devote to horticultural pursuits; or if my wife insists —and when she does insist she insists pretty strongly —I can retire to town with my investment trebled."

Results of Inquiry.

I HAVE thus brought to view through the vehicle of an imaginary examination—and in the interest of my friend Mr. Urban, and similar inquirers—all the aspects of a fifty-acre farm purchased at the East, with which I am familiar. The inquiry as herein set forth, may possibly help him to an intelligible decision.

There may be learned from it, I think—First: that with unlimited means, and the simple wish to lavish them in country employments, it matters very little where a man may establish himself, or what special whim he adopts—whether for fine cattle, or horticultural successes; but he may be assured that he will win no confirmed triumph in either one or the other, without having a personal love for the business and a knowledge of it, or without employing, invariably, those who do have such love or knowledge.

Second : it may be fairly inferred that a fifty-acre purchase is not necessarily a bad affair, even if the purchaser is not personally competent to direct operations, provided he has the shrewdness to avail himself of the experience and good common-sense of those who have the competency.

Third : it may be learned that all the theories about drainage, and particularly breeds, and the blasting away of rocky fastnesses, and the use of concentrated manures will avail nothing, except they be under the direction, and subject to the execution of a thoroughly practical man, who has an eye to sale as well as purchase, and to crop as well as tillage. Philosophers, at best, make doubtful farmers : but adventurous philosophers whose brains bristle with theories, and who are without that breadth of knowledge which enables a man to compare theory with theory and understand remote as well as immediate relations, make the worst farmers it is possible to imagine. I have a high regard for our agricultural newspapers, and think they are doing far more good than our agricultural colleges (as developed thus far); but there are weaklings, who, finding support from a

newspaper correspondent for some ill-digested theory
of their own, leap to monstrous conclusions.

Fourth : the inquiries will show that a shrewd,
old-fashioned farmer—no matter where his land may
lie—may make fifty acres yield fair return, and not
involve inordinate expenditure. True, very possibly,
that such as my friend Mr. Urban do not wish to live
as Mr. Sloman lived, or to labor as he labored; but his
report (which may be well substantiated) is a fair
indication of the possibilities of fifty-acre farming.

Fifth : it is clearly enough demonstrated that
however inapt a man may be at farming or horticultural pursuits, if he have the business forecast to
make purchase of land near to a growing centre of
population, his pecuniary success is made sure. There
is indeed a sort of commercial genius—of low rank it
may be—which consists in simply holding on to land
when the tide of population surges around it, and the
" offers " beat like waves upon it, and spend a great
spray of promise over it.

In view of all these " findings " Mr. Urban cannot surely be at a loss to regulate his determination.
If his means are large, (as largeness is counted nowadays,) and he has a love for fine cattle of best blood,
let him—anywhere he will,—import the best animals,
look to their rearing, and he may establish a herd
that will carry away the premiums and give him

reputation, if they give him no profit. Great reputation may go without great profit, though great profit hardly ever goes, in our time, without great reputation.

If he have a fancy for architectural and other decorations, it may safely be said that fifty acres will furnish ample margin for the most riotous expenditure. It is quite amazing indeed—as much to the proprietor as outsiders—to witness the voracity with which a small place even—under elegant and misguided direction—will consume moneys. The engrossing tastes of the city are not without a capability in this direction; but one or two good sandbanks, a small ledge, a plantation, and artificial ponds —in connection with a rural taste which is ambitious without being experienced, will I think absorb money as easily as any outlets of the metropolis.

I should strongly counsel Mr. Urban, or any other, who feels this inclination possessing him, thoroughly to mature his plans before beginning; there is no rural wasting so monstrous as the waste of building walls and removing them, or of excavating valleys and the next summer filling them up. A few judicious hints at the beginning, based on good sense and taste combined, may work the saving of thousands. I am inclined to think that the pleasant scenes of the Central Park are to be credited (or charged) with a great deal of riotous or ineffective private expenditure: those who have gleaned all their knowledge of landscape-gardening from that out-of-door school—a very charming one in many of its features—have left out of consideration the fact, that public expenditure knows no economies, and an army of lazy laborers, dragging at the bosom of the public treasury, may keep in presentable shape the walks and drives which would be ruin to a private holder. The rule of action, as of taste, in public parks, is, to produce the best effects at inordinate cost: the whole question of economy, whether of establishment or future treatment, is eliminated from discussion. With private holders, on the other hand, the great question is,—what effects may be produced at a minimum of cost for their establishment, and at a minimum of cost for their future annual keeping.

For these reasons, I think the ruralist who meditates a repetition of a bit of the Central Park upon his grounds, will sink fearfully in the mire of costs and of mud. There are charming features in the Park undoubtedly, but the charming things are, most of them, underlaid with gold, and will be found to require a golden watering for a long time to come.

Again, if Mr. Urban or any other farm adventurer has his chemical or other hobbies which he wishes to carry out, let him not count implicitly upon his power to uproot in a season all the practices of centuries. There is an obstinacy (after all) in God's soil and seed-beds which humiliates the wittiest lecturers or the best adepts at the retort. If he be thoroughly infected, I only counsel modest expectations—a proper humanity toward his working cattle, and the ordinary business foresight of keeping a good balance at his bank when the bills come in.

If he has neither short-horn nor landscape ambition, and is not infected with any mania of drainage, or peat, or Liebig—wishing only the grateful shade from trees not subject to the visitations of the curculio, and a sweet bowl of milk to his supper, let him not be too eager to discard the offices of those old-style farmers, who, if not adepts in culture, are adepts in saving.

Finally, if his rural fantasy is only a short-lived whim that may pass one day—if not from his own mind, at least from the more sensitive and demonstrative mind of his help-meet—let him buy where he can sell. He may be sure that the trees will lose none of the pleasantness of their leafy rustle if it be spent on ears that listen more eagerly than his own. His porches, his arbors, his walks, his fields will entertain him none the less, if covetous eyes look over the fence at them. There may be something very wicked, but there is something very human in

11*

the cheerfulness with which we watch people breaking the tenth commandment.   Horace has touched
the matter prettily in his satire ; but he might have
added that the merchant is never so contented, as
when he hears the old soldier, or the officer on half-
pay exclaim : " *O fortunati mercatores !* "   And the
country is never more charming than when we read
—and reading, believe—

> " Agricolam laudat juris legumque peritus."

When Mr. Urban shall have made the skilful
lawyer covetous of his fruits, his fields, his walks, he
may sell—if he chooses.   As I said, we never cease
breaking the tenth commandment and trying to make
other people break it.   And pray, who keeps the
other nine ?

Country Houses and Repairs.

WHAT man or woman of us all does not some
time think of a house that shall one day be a
home ?   Who does not ponder the subject—forecast
its details—outline its surroundings—invest it with
charms—dally with its image, and give to his imagin-
ings a most grateful acceptance ?   For my own
part, I think I began to build, when as yet I stood in
daily fear of the ferule of a school-mistress, and
when, under a knitted Scotch school-cap, there came

into my brain a delicious jumble of porches and gables and broad roofs dabbled over with the sunlight and the shadows. I cannot doubt but that very many others have had much the same experience.

There is a class indeed (not very large, I should hope) of both men and women, always afloat, who find all their home appetites in those great caravansaries which we call hotels, and whose local attachments must be of a very vague and illusory character: but I cannot fancy such among my readers— first, because these have no leisure to listen to what I may say; and next, because their sympathies must be altogether remote from the topics I discuss. I address myself rather to those who have some day had thoughts of building houses of their own, and who have invested the thought with a thousand homely fancies.

A low, gray, irregular range of buildings with a multitude of gables, and here and there a turret lifting above them—broad windows blazing in the sunlight, and windows darkened with trailing festoons of some wall-creeper—an ample hall of entrance, with quaint stairway climbing to some landing lit with an oriel—a blue chamber, a green chamber, an oak chamber—rambling corridors opening upon yet other chambers—a great dim garret with the sunlight flashing in through some dormer window upon roof-beams hung with dried herbs and gone-by clothing and wreck of discarded furniture—porches that invite and protect and throw welcome shadows on the door— little mantling rooflets of windows that temper the glare of day, and at dusk break the dark mass of building with picturesque outlying angles : I think I have indicated some of the features which belong to most people's ideal of a country home. But who makes them real ? who reaches their ideal in any thing—whether in home, in reputation, or success of any sort ?

But as regards the country home, what is in the way ? We will suppose that our friend Mr. Urban has possessed himself at last of the fifty acres he sought for ; there is wood, there is water, there are meadows, and withal there is an old farm-house, the home of the out-going owner, with its clumps of lilacs, its bunches of syringa, its encompassing mat of green sward. Its site is not, may be, precisely the one that he would have chosen ; but the poor drag- gled bit of shrubbery and the mossy cherry-trees that stand near give to it a pleasant homeliness of aspect, with which any new site with its raw upturned gravels and fresh-planted shrubs must for a long time contrast very painfully. Thus the question comes up —more appealingly every day he looks on it, Will not the old hulk do with a little modernizing ? And the thought of putting a new, jaunty look upon the old tame outline of building, has something in it that is very captivating.

This suggests our first topic of discussion—Is it wise to undertake the repair of an old country house? The builder or the architect, eager for a fat job, will say no: the mistress, with a settled distaste for low ceilings and wavy floors that tell fearfully upon the carpets, will say no: but a practical man will be guided in his decision by the condition of the building, and by the range of the proposed changes. Two or three axioms in connection with this subject it may be worth while to bear in mind. First: it is never quite possible to make an altogther new house out of an old one. Second: it is the most difficult thing in the world to determine in advance the cost or limit of the proposed repairs to an old country house. Third: it is altogether impossible to say in advance that any system of change, however deliberately considered, will prove ultimately satisfactory to the (female) occupants.

These truisms would seem to count against the undertaking to remodel an old house: yet there are conditions which make it eminently wise, as well in a practical as in an æsthetic point of view.

If, for instance, the walls be of stone or brick, and not wholly inconsiderable in extent, it would be bad

economy as well as bad taste to sacrifice them to any
craving for newness. In the brick, if well laid, a
man may be sure of stanchness; and in the stone,
with the lichens of years upon it, he has a mellowness
of tone which not all the arts of the decorators can
reach. But even upon walls of such material, especially if they carry the blotches of age, it will
never do to engraft the grandiose designs of the
modern builders. If a country liver be really ambitious to match all the pretensions of the latest architecture in respect of high ceilings and mansard-roofs,
let him begin by pulling down; but if his aim be of
that finer temper which seeks to qualify what is old
by enlargement of dimensions and by such simple
decorative features as shall add a piquancy to the
wrinkles of age—even as the twist of some sober-
colored ribbon will set off some be-capped and wid-
owed face more attractively than all the snow-flake
haberdashery that could be devised—let him cherish
all the quaintness that is due to years, and seek only
to magnify and illustrate it by such enlargements as
are in keeping with it, and by such sober adornments
as shall seem to be rather a restoration of old and lost
graces than the ambitious display of new ones. The
thing is feasible. It only wants an eye to perceive
the need, and a courage to discard the flash carpentry
of the day.

I beg that I may be not misunderstood. I by no means intend to say that the country houses of fifty years ago were in any sense equal or comparable, on the score of fitness or of taste, to the country houses of to-day; but I do mean to say, that if the walls of such old houses are *plumb* and true and sound, and repairs are undertaken, it will be far wiser, and call for nicer exercise of skill, to carry forward such repairs with the quaint flavor of the old homely tastes upon them—thus working out artistic agreement and adornment together—than it will be to belittle the old by a shocking contrast, and wantonly dress our grandame in the furbelows of sixteen.

Again, let me lay down another distinction. There are old houses which, in any traditional or artistic sense, are *not* old houses. They are mere square boxes of lumber or stone, without noticeable feature or flavor. Such, if posssible, may be incorporated into any new design, without fear or favor; none but economic considerations will stand in the way. But there are others which, without being accordant in any sense with the artistic designs of the present day, have yet a character of their own—a character which any architectural adviser (by the qualities of his profession) is bound to detect; and which (by the niceties of his profession) he cannot ignore in carrying out his changes.

I know of nothing which an architect can do
better (in the way of illustrating his real artistic
capacity) than to take hold of one of those old, almost
uninhabitable country houses of forty years ago, and,
without violating its homeliness, graft upon it such
convenient addenda of rooms, porches, halls (gables,
possibly) as shall result in a charming homestead,
in which the old is forgotten in the new, and the
new made racy by a certain indefinable smack of the
old.

For all such renovation, however, as I have hinted
at, stanch walls and sound timbers are essential pre-
requisites. If otherwise—if the examining carpenter
can thrust his scratch-awl eight inches into the sills—
if the posts have taken gradual settlement and the
ceiling shows gaping rents, any effective remodelling
must be of doubtful conomy. Of course there must
be a substitution of new sills, and a splicing of the
posts which will make even wider gaps in the ceiling.
Then comes the pleasant suggestion of the *mater
familias* that the mantels are awkward and must be
replaced by something new and tasteful. The adroit
mason, being called into consultation, decides that the
chimneys are hardly worth the change, and that a
renovation from top to bottom would give a large
addition of closet room. So the old chimneys come
down, with such dirt and breakage and necessary

removal of partition walls as are surprising. The
ceilings, too, must needs show ugly patches, and it
would be wiser (the amiable mason suggests) to re-
plaster altogether. There must be new hearths too,
and in place of an awkward patched floor perhaps it
would be better to renew the flooring. This being
undertaken, it is found that the sleepers are awry,
and to make square work the carpenter suggests a
replacement of the flooring timber. This being
accomplished, it is hinted by the observant mistress
that the windows are hardly in keeping, and the
order is given for new frames and sashes. The
doors must needs match the windows; and next
there is a sly regret that the plain ceilings should not
have their fretting of a town cornice: and so the
poor old house is gradually dwarfed with a great
burden of pretentious modernisms that it can carry
with no grace. Even the *mater familias* has at last
her disappointments, and says quietly: " Sylvanus (it
is of Mr. Urban that I write), I think 'twould have
been perhaps better to build a new house."

Unquestionably.

Site and Material.

BUT if new, what is to be said of site, of material,
of style? Not absolutely upon a hill-top, I
should say, unless there be some great flanking wood

against the north, or such planting and arrangement
of outbuildings as shall presently secure shelter : not
upon low land either—least of all near to any body
of fresh water which from artificial causes is subject
to great inequalities of level, or which in the heats
of September may show a broad margin of quagmire.
Lakes are very beautiful, and very healthful too, as
God made them ; but when the manufacturers or the
water companies tap them, as they will most persistently in the seasons of least rain, all their charm and
glory go sounding down the sluices.

One would say too that a model country house or
an enjoyable one should be placed upon such lift of
ground as to give a good honest out-look over meadow and wood, and streaks of river (if such can be
compassed).   The near sight of the roofs and towers
of a city, too, will give a good every-day feeling of
companionship with the world, without the world's
noises ; and I am not sure but that a spire or two
lifting above trees or among trees will breed a
healthful religious habit in a man—shining always in
his eye—trim, solid sermons—not smirched with the
dust of groundling conflicts, and (unlike many written
sermons) always carrying a good point in them.
There should be also some glimpse, if nothing more,
of one of the world's great highways ; a near railway
is indeed terrific with its din, but if so far away

that its roar is mellowed by distance, the arrowy
flight of its trains gives a pleasant bit of movment to
the landscape. Best of all, for picturesque effect, is
the feathery trail of white vapor which the rattling
monster breathes out and which lies floating after
him like a line of mist over the whole breadth of the
valley-crossing. Such objects as I have indicated forbid that feeling of solitude which steals upon one
immured in a scene of absolute retirement. Trees
are never less than trees indeed, and mountains are
always writ over with grand lines ; but after all, it
is a weary silence that only birds break or the mono-
tone of frogs or the locusts. An echo from without,
whether from a bell-tower or the sweep of a railway
train, is a sort of brazen world's voice booming in,
that by contrast makes the bird's notes sweeter, and
the leafy rustle of the trees more beguiling.

Of the material of which a country house should
be constructed I shall say some things which are not
in agreement with prevailing opinions. The use of
wood is almost universal ; and for producing a certain
largeness of effect under limitations of cost, it is by
odds the most economical. The necessary conditions
too of warmth and dryness may be easily secured by
a builder in wood ; and under these circumstances,
where fitness and economy seem combined, it is
hardly reasonable to hope for the substitution of any

other material than wood. Yet I venture to suggest, (and shall urge as I best can,) that in a country where stones abound, and they abound in most of the Eastern States, they furnish the most fit material, and their use will subserve a higher if not a more immediate economy.

Let me test, one by one, the objections which are commonly urged against buildings for home purposes, of stone.

First, on the score of appearance: There are those who object to the rough and unbecoming particolored surface of a house of stone—who believe that a " handsome house " (a most destestable collocation of words) must have smooth exteriors, and submit to the finical niceties of the painters. This, indeed, is a question of taste, in which all ordinary reasoning is adrift. It certainly seems to me that the real beauty of a country house depends not so much upon nice finish of surface as upon outline, and the agreement of its general tone of color with the surrounding landscape. No tint, surely, can be more agreeable than that of our sand-stones, and the yellow ochreous stain which belongs to the old cleavage of the trap-rock is as rich as that of the quarries of Caen. Then there is the lichened surface of a world of scattered boulders—their fresh bright cleavage with its spangles of mica, or the homely brown weather stains of myriads of dispersed fragments. And even if agreement of tint be wanting, it is quite feasible to build of wholly refuse stones in such way as to admit of a " rough-cast " covering of mortar, which by the simple appliance of lime-wash and some cheap pigment, may be toned to any color desired : or, by selection of stones for the quoins and window jambs, these might show their natural surfaces, while the intervals were " rough-cast." A kindred though more decided contrast of color might be secured by quoins and window trimmings of brick, while the general surface (sunk two or three inches) might be treated as already suggested. By these devices the rudest stones might be worked into a solid home.

Another method, in which comparatively worthless material may be utilized in the construction of a house, which would have all the warmth and nearly all the durability of a building wholly of stone, is to blend the timber and mason-work together—framing as usual, though with a nice regard to joints and effective panelling, and after this, building in with coarse rubble, to be rough-cast on completion, leaving the timbers exposed. This is the old Saxon country house, of which many examples are to be found in the cathedral cities of England, and of which the Shakespeare house is a notable but very humble type.

Instances of this mode of construction are not common in this country—scarcely known indeed at the North; but quaint specimens are to be seen in Louisiana and in Florida. By the favor of a friend, I introduce a little sketch of a very modest building of this sort in the neighborhood of New Orleans.

I am sure that something larger might be done in this way, which would have a very racy quaintness; and which, with its timber balcony and jutting rooflets and ample porches might offer a very inviting show.

Brick may also be used effectively for the filling in of such exposed carpentry of the frame; and if such timber be given a dark chocolate tint, the contrast is very striking and pleasing.

I give a sketch of such a house, with the addition

of a mansard roof and a basement of quarry
chips.

Aside from those who object to the appearance of a
stone house, there are many who entertain the very

current prejudice that such buildings must needs be damp. If damp, the dampness must be due to faulty construction. Nothing more is needed to secure dryness than to " fur off" widely from the stone, and to allow a free circulation of air between the interior and exterior walls. In this way not only is dryness secured, but a degree of warmth in winter, and of coolness in summer, which no wooden walls can maintain. In this connection it may be worth while to note the fact, that the larger part of the civilized portion of the world have been living in stone houses for the last few centuries, and they have weathered the damps pretty courageously.

But the objection to country houses of stone is not so much on the score of appearance or of imagined dampness, as of cost. The great durability is hardly taken into our American estimates. There are rural householders who look forward twenty years—some who look forward fifty years; but those who look forward a century and build for the generations to come, may be counted on one's fingers. What builder of our day reckons upon the wants or comforts of his grand-child ? What boy counts upon living in his father's house ? There are exceptions, doubtless, but the rule is, dispersion—sale—alienation; and not one man in a thousand is shaded by the oaks that gave shelter to his grandsire. If I build a house which is in sound and saleable condition forty or fifty years hence, what more is needed ?

But even under this short-sighted view, is the house of wood more economical than the house of stone ? If, as I have hinted, the projector aims at a finical nicety of exterior surface, there can be no question that economy is largely in favor of the use of wood ; but if a man will have the courage to violate conventional tastes in this respect, and be content, nay, be boastful of a rural residence—if it offer only agreeable outline and afford ample security for all comfort and elegance within, there is a large doubt if stone, if readily accessible, be not the more economic material. A large allowance in its favor is to be made in view of the fact that the painters' bills must needs be modest, and that repairs for an indefinite series of years will be almost infinitesimal. And yet whatever may be a man's plottings in favor of rude material, and a resolute indifference to other beauty of exterior than the natural faces of the scattered boulders in his fields, it is quite possible that the city masons, if consulted, will swell their estimates to the same aggregate that belongs to the nice finish of the town houses. Every experiment, even in the direction of economy, is taxed somewhat by reason of its quality of experiment.

To avoid this tax it would be well to seek out

12

some trusty and sagacious foreman who could be brought to entertain some pride in the issue of the proposed scheme and allow him to select the laborers through whom it should be carried into execution on "day's wages." Good country wall-layers, who have only a little deftness in the use of the trowel, would be capital co-workers; and at all hazards, that riffraff of lazy fellows should be discarded who delight in hammering out ten listless hours in defacement of the beautiful natural cleavage of our rocks.

Another matter worthy of full consideration is the fact that the cost of a stone house increases rapidly with its height; the first twelve feet may be easily manageable, but the next twelve involve portentous array of scaffolding, and the lifting of large masses of material: economy would thus seem to dictate, where stone is employed, low walls and a large area. Would our country houses lose in picturesqueness or in comfort by such a readjustment of proportions?

Form and Color.

THIS leads me to speak of form. The man who goes up two flights of stairs every night in the country to his bed, does a very preposterous thing.

If not two, why go up one? A large compensation of country life lies in the possession of space: no brick wall flanks your rear; no neighbor's area lies under your dining-room windows; ample stretch of ground for all architectural fancies surrounds and invites you. Why not improve it? Does character lie in tallness? The old Romans—those luxurious comfort-seekers—understood the charm that lay in a *cubiculum*, if not a *dormitorium* on the first floor; and with a door half open (such doors as they had) they might go to sleep, lulled by the tinkle of a fountain in the hall. I don't think any of Pliny's villas were as high as those of a great many (in sight from my door) who don't know whether he was Greek or Chinaman.

Of course we don't want, in this age of the world, to take our building fancies from the dead men of Pompeii or of Tusculum; and I have only interpolated this allusion to show that a man's dignity is not necessarily measured by the height of the house he lives in. All the strong, robber classes of the world, whenever they have lived in houses, have, I think, inclined to tall ones. Such were those German barons who perched their eyries along the Rhine, and the thievish borderers by the Tweed who have left us such precious specimens as " Johnny Armstrong's Tower." On the other hand, the domesticity of the old Saxons expressed itself in low, wide-spreading buildings, typical of a quiet life, and of a country abundance that came by peaceful labor.

There are robber classes in our day, and they live (many of them) in tall houses ; so do a great many nonest people, for that matter. In fact a great fault of our country architecture lies in its being too ambitious : it has indeed come out from that old hideous conventionalism of two stories, white clap-boards and green blinds ; but it still seeks to startle with something grand—something that shall tell a noisy brazen story at the first glance. Yet a fit house and home—fit for its belongings—fit in size, in color, in outline (like a man of wholly fit character)—should win upon you by degrees, charming you at each succeeding look by some rare and modest beauties, which are the more attractive because found only after intelligent search. A great, gaunt, cumbrous exterior tells all its story at a glance : you may study it curiously in search of details, but there is no hearty interest in the study. But a humbler line of roof, so humble that we catch sight bit by bit of its peeping gables, its jutting porches, its low flanking line of offices—half hid by shrubbery and half warmed by a blaze of sunlight—this, somehow, by a certain relishy smack of domesticity belonging to its vague indistinguishable outline and scattered chimney-stacks, piques all the home-feeling in a man.

A great house, whose picture we have seen in the architectural books, we know; and we admire it coldly, if we admire it at all. But a lesser one—less

beautiful, possibly, judged by the conventional laws of the art—whose quaint assemblage of modest peaks and outlying offices seems to shadow forth the individuality of the occupant, and is invested with a homely yet cheery quietude—this we admire with a livelier interest.

If, however, economy in the use of stone for domestic purposes demands comparatively low walls, it need not cheat us wholly of our chambers. A French roof, with great perpendicularity to its first pitch, will give airy height for upper rooms and ample ventilating space above; and such a roof, slated in diamond pattern, will contrast admirably with the natural surfaces of the boulders below, and the irregular lines of mortar.

Again, I do not know anything in the laws of taste, apart from conventionalisms, to which we all yield so implicitly, which would forbid the placing of an upper story of wooden construction upon a ground-story of stone. The idea may be shocking at first, but I ask the reader to fancy for a moment an irregular mass of honest stone building of the height and simplicity I have suggested, pierced with windows of irregular proportions (just where needed for the best light). Next imagine a wooden structure of a story in height, with simple sharp pent roof, relieved by a gable half down its length, placed upon the stone—overhanging it if you please by a foot in width and length, with its floor timbers rounded into the shape of supporting corbels; then imagine here and there a half-dozen of these floor-beams projecting four feet or more, so as to form a dainty balcony at

some upper window, supported by simple timber braces carried down into the stone-work; others may project still further, to carry the peaked rooflet of a porch, whose supporting posts shall reach the ground; the wooden covering may be of sheathing arranged vertically, tinted brown to harmonize with the stone, and the battens of whitish gray to harmonize with the mortar lines below. The professional men might call this very inelegant; but I am not sure that strict artistic elegance is the best quality for a home in the country. The best qualities in it will be those that call out most promptly a man's sense of domesticity—that suggest easy comfort, ample room, odd loitering nooks, indefinite play of fire-light and lamp-light, wide and unpretentious hospitality. Above all things a country house, to have its best charm, must look *livable*. I use an exceptionable word, but I think readers will catch my meaning. The mere suggestion—such as tightly-closed shutters will give—of rooms kept for show, barred for weeks and months against light and air, will ruin its charm. Its walls, windows, roof, chimneys, must beam with cheeriness. Its porch must nod a welcome. A terrier frisking through a half-opened door, a cat dozing on a balcony, a dove swooping round the gable, will lend more charms by odds than carefully swept gravel and a statue of Diana on the lawn. There must be no stiff pairing of circle against circle, or of hanging basket against hanging basket—above all, no such execrable tom-foolery as iron dogs or wooden puppets. A Grecian temple for a coal shed, or a small Strasburg minster for a dog-house, will help largely to make a country house absurd. Nay, an excess of nicety upon the walks, as if the spade and roller of the gardener left it only yesterday and would be there again next morning, takes off the edge of a true home relish; even flowers themselves, if piled up in very trim and very orderly masses, as in the show-rows of a florist, will lose half their power to lend grace; still worse if they are perched in soldierly array along the porch or veranda, renewed so soon as their bloom fades, like children never allowed to appear even in party dress save under promise of keeping still. Who, pray, can take comfort in lounging upon a porch, where a careless step may break off some floweret of a rare cactus, or enjoy a bit of greens-ward where he fears to knock off the ashes of his cigar? Who wants to be petrified in a country house, either his own or another's? I have seen them before now so terribly fine, so prudishly neat, so martinet-like in order, that it seemed to me the very gardeners should be wearing leathern stocks and pipe-clay: a week of such atmosphere would drive me mad.

Perhaps I am peculiar in these notions about the

12*

real *homishness* of a country place. I know there
are very good and Christian people who never allow
a dog about their premises, or a duck, or a dove, or
a stray dandelion upon their lawn, and who buy
statuary and rustic iron work (always in pairs) for
their grounds, and who keep the front blinds closed,
and who manage to give to their sunniest porch the
look of a church door upon week-days; but why
such people should come into the country or live in
the country I could never understand. It puzzles me
prodigiously.

I like hugely that good old English word—homeliness. It ought to have again its first meaning.
Pretty-faced women have corrupted it. It describes
all that is best about a country house. I have ad-
vocated the use of homely material and of homely
methods, believing these are best fitted judiciously
used, to lend real homeliness to a house in the
country.

Mr. Urban's Purchase.

MR. URBAN has at last positively succeeded in
making purchase of his farm of fifty acres, or
thereabout. It has its undulations, its scattered woods,
its obtruding cliff—in short, a sufficiently varied surface to admit of a certain picturesque treatment,

without great interference with economic results. For Mr. Urban is bent upon having his cornpatch—however much it may cost him; and bent upon having his trim lines of carrots, his mercers, his half dozen or more of fine cattle, and his pasturage, where he may watch his Alderneys at their quiet grazing, or their noontide siesta under the trees.

I give, on the next page, a drawing of his farm as it appeared at the time of his taking possession.

The house, *A*, is reasonably sound, and well situated, but small. It will admit of temporary repairs and additions, which he determines upon forthwith. The barn, *B*, is wholly unfit for his plans, being small, ill-placed, and shaky in its joints. He consults me in regard to the position for a new one, and I advise him to place it in the edge of the mossy old orchard (whose trees are nearly worthless), where a little rise of ground will admit of a cellar underneath both barn and carriage-house. I suggest also in connection with it a cow-stable which shall extend westward in order to furnish a protecting lee to his cattle-yard, and to connect immediately with the fields in the rear.

The fences are terrible in number, but are fortunately nearly all of rails, and can therefore be placed out of consideration in the new laying out of

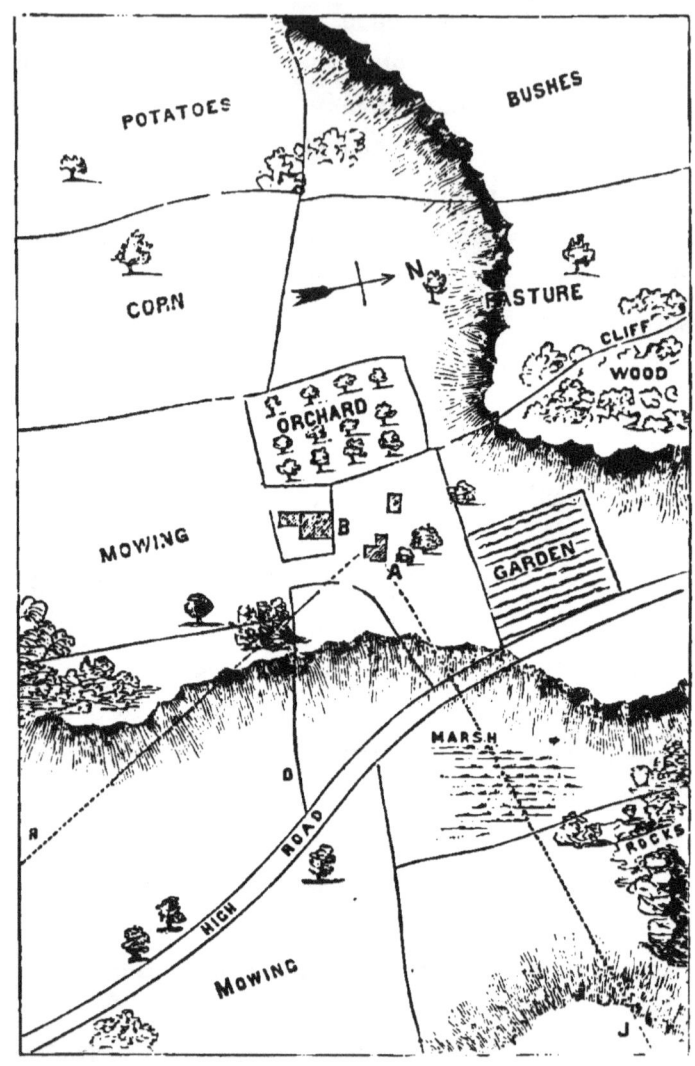

the farm. An exception is to be noted in regard
to the line of enclosure marked *O* upon the diagram,

which—as well as the fences along either side of the
high-road—are of old mossy boulders, too cumbrous
to be removed without great cost. Mistress Urban
is in despair at this, as she thinks that the particular fence designated will prevent any breadth to
her lawn. In the interests of economy, however, I
venture to advise that it be left in its present position—that it be righted where it shows any bulging
propensities, and promise that in two or three years
at most the greater part of it shall be screened by
irregular groups of shrubbery, and that where its
line is discernible, it shall be mantled with such a
tangled wealth of Virginia creepers and ivy (the
exposure being north) as shall make it worthy its
place, and divide admiration with the half dozen of
mouse-colored Alderneys feeding beyond.

The garden is out of position, besides being upon
a soil ill suited to it. Mr. Urban is moreover urgent
for a " great garden ; " he wishes to prepare one in
the best manner, and means that his standard pears
and dwarf fruits and grapevines shall come in for a
share of the benefit.

I establish it upon the level plateau of land to the
southward of his cattle-yard, giving it the advantage
of shelter from the stables, the cold grapery, the
compost-shed, the hot-house and the hennery—as
will appear by consulting the second drawing of

Mr. Urban's fifty acres, after the improvements are matured.

The cold grapery is marked *F';* the hot-house, *E,* whose fire, by proper adjustment of one of its flues, gives warmth to the poultry-house, which (marked *D*) is immediately adjoining. A sheltered spot for hot-bed and compost-heap is provided in a position convenient to the manure deposits of the cattle-yard. A broad walk, at least eight feet in width, traverses the garden, and divides near the southern border, to give place to a picturesque coppice of trees and shrubs, whose interior border is planted with hardy and showy herbaceous flowers; these again are hemmed in every summer-time by a narrower and exterior border of the gayest of " bedding " plants. Behind, and to the southward of the garden paling or hedge is a green lane, serving to connect the pasture-land by the high-road, with the cultivated lands to the westward, and with the stable court. This connection may be established, while the west lands are under tillage, by means of a hurdle fence, which shall extend the lane along the west border of the garden.

The fields marked *M* and *R* are, as expressed upon the diagram, either in tillage or in meadow; and the multitude of fences has been done away with. The southernmost of these two fields is laid bare for thorough tillage of any character, and its neighbor to the north has only a protecting belt of wood.

The enclosure K, having a ledge and an old group of forest trees in its northwestern angle (offering admirable shelter), may have its picturesquely disposed orcharding, or may be planted with ornamental trees, as the proprietor may fancy. In either case, with a few protective hurdles, it may be cropped by a score of Southdowns; but it must be fairly understood that no orcharding will do its best or even its second best, except it be kept under thorough cultivation, and no grass permitted within reach of its most divergent rootlets.

The walks and entrance drive explain themselves. The dotted line H I, indicates a view of a distant village spire, which upon the first diagram, as will be seen, was entirely cut off by two or three intruding trees; and even when these were removed, the view was sadly interfered with by the mossy wall already spoken of. To obviate this difficulty I suggested a gap in the wall thereabout, and the establishment of a broad rustic gate under whose rude arch the distant spire would come into sight as through a frame-work. A rough sketch will give a hint of the vista.

No pencilling, however, will represent that soft suffusion of smoky color which enwraps the little spire and house-roofs, as they come to the eye through the gap in the sharp dark green of the foreground.

The view to the northeast (in the direction of the dotted line *J*), at the time of taking possession, looked over a foul marsh lying upon the opposite side of the high-road; this marsh received the drainage of all

the elevated ground to the north and west, and its excess of water leaked away by an indecisive and intermittent flow through the pasture land marked *P*. Under the old regime—as will be seen by recurrence to the drawing of the farm at time of purchase —this pasture served as " meadow," and produced its annual quota of bog hay. Beyond the marsh and the highlands which skirted it to the northeast, was an extremely pretty view of a range of low mountains, some two miles distant, in the lee of which were to be seen a spire and one or two tall chimneys. But the unkempt, slatternly marsh-land in the foreground ruined the scene. It might be planted out indeed; but an effective planting out would interfere

somewhat with some of the most picturesque objects
in the distance. I advised a slight excavation of a
portion of the marsh so as to show a little lakelet,
over whose farther arm a rustic bridge might be
thrown—the bridge serving as a portion of the barrier between the area of *plaisance* ground around the
pond and the pasture beyond. By this device and
adroit disposition of shrubbery, the whole area south
of the high-road would appear from the windows of
the mansion to constitute but one enclosure, within
which the pet Alderneys might be seen cropping the
herbage, or cooling themselves in the pool beyond
the bridge.

Of course such disposition of the matter (which
I have tried to illustrate in the drawing) commended

itself most warmly to Mrs. Urban and to the Misses
Urbans. Nor did the *pater familias* greatly object.

To add still more to the picturesqueness of this

view across the road, I proposed the introduction of
the gardener's cottage upon the wayside, in such manner that its quaint gable should peep from the trees
upon the right of the scene, and a well-trimmed hedge
of hemlock shut out all sight of the road-way. The
diagram already given will show the position of the
water, the walks, the gardener's cottage, and the
gardener's patch of vegetables—this latter being
quite out of sight from the high grounds by the mansion.

It is quite essential to the effectiveness of this
design for the lay-out of the grounds that the public
road be kept in neat and trim condition—so neat and
so trim that the visitor approaching it from the south
(the direction of the nearest railway station), shall,
when he arrives opposite the gardener's cottage
(whose porch must jut upon the highway), involun-
tarily reckon it a gate-lodge of some private domain
into which he just there enters. For the fuller
establishment of this pleasant deceit, the real entrance
gates should be of the simplest and most unpretending character—as if they were but portions of some
interior enclosures. Whatever grass or shrubs may
grow within the public road after passing the gardener's cottage should be as zealously cared for and
as trimly kept as if they were within the enclosing
wall. One may be assured that the neighboring

public will never resent such careful keeping of the high-road, and they may be brought by it, in time to practise some such picturesque devices on their own account.

Another hint I think it necessary to drop here. The lay-out of a place upon paper it is easy to make very engaging and tasteful; there is indeed no limit to the graces of curve, which may be laid down by an adroit draftsman upon a fair sheet of Bristol board. But it is a very different matter to establish the same graces upon the land itself. Unlimited expenditure may indeed make any surface conform itself to the curvatures and devices of a drawing. But the art of arts in landscape gardening is to make outlay illustrate the beauties of the land, and not to cramp and deplete the land to illustrate the charms of the drawing.

Particular curves or undulations of surface, which may have a most attractive look in a finished landscape, may lack very many of the essentials of grace if transferred to paper, after the ordinary manner of topographical drawing. If we looked at landscape effects always from a balloon—if the hills were all fore-shortened, and the curves of walks or drives all determinable at a glance, a ground map would be a very fair guide by which to determine artistic effects. But the truth is that in nature the hills have their perspective; the scattered trees or coppices are not mere woolly blotches, but slant their shadows upon the surface and toss their tops into the sky-line; curves are not cognizable in their length, or ease, or abruptnesses at a glance—we steal upon them by degrees; they please by their easy cheatery—by their unexpected sequence—by such abrupt diversions, even, as have palpable cause in inequality of surface or obtruding rock or cliff. It is quite possible, indeed—nay, it is altogether probable that the curves and devices which are most charmingly effective in the work itself, may have a stiffness and an impertinence upon the map which will thoroughly disappoint.

As cases in point, I remember once looking down with exceeding interest from the height of some Italian town (I think in Bologna) upon what seemed a charming garden; its curves were full of grace; its little coppices were admirably adjusted; its flow of walks as happy as a dream; but when I found my way to it afterward, by a bribe to its custodian, and met it upon tame level—the bird's-eye view being gone—it seemed the baldest of dreary pattern-work in turf—with no significance in its curves, and no keeping in its lines.

Again, there was a day when I went wandering in sun and shadow through the masses of a Scotch garden, not far from Hawthornden, with cliff and brook and water and bridge and tangles of wildwood—all so caught by the landscape designer and so strung along the foot-ways he had planted, that delight was unceasing; and when I asked for a sketch of its meandering over that broken surface, it presented such an array of tame lines, and meaningless curvatures and violent crooks as to express nothing of the grace which on the grounds themselves flowed over, and made constant enchantment.

A Sunny House.

WE will suppose that Mr. Urban is thoroughly satisfied with his garden and grounds—that he finds his newly planted trees growing apace—that his Southdowns are all that an accomplished grazier could desire; but the old house becomes at last a weariness. Not because it is old; nor yet because it is comparatively small—so small that he has to billet, from time to time, a bachelor visitor in a little loft of his tool-house; but it has no wide and open frontage to the sun. He insists that the new one, of which he projects the building out of the rough material from his cliff, shall have at least a glimpse of southern sunshine in every habitable room below.

" I am tired of the gloom of north exposures," he writes ; " wood-fires are very well, but the blaze of them is not equal to the blaze of sunshine. Do what you will with the north side, but the parlor must look to the south, and the library (of course) and the dining-room, and—without going up-stairs—there must, if possible, be a billiard-room and a bed-room, looking the same sunny way. In brief, my notion is, to have a house with plenty of room, and no north side to it. Can the problem be solved ?

" I don't care for shape, if it be only picturesque, and meet the wants I have named above. A considerable slope of the land toward the west upon the locality I have chosen, (keeping all the old charming views in leash) will admit of an airy basement at the western end, and full windows (two of them) to the south. This would furnish a good spot for billiards, if you can contrive a respectable stairway down from the hall ; and if the billiard-room opens out westwardly into a special conservatory, where one can smoke his cigar to kill the red spiders (or green ones, I forget which), all the better.

" What on earth you will do with the north side of the house under this ruling of windows and wants, I don't know. I should say a long picture-gallery, if I had pictures. What if it were to be a blank wall with ivies growing over it ? But then there's the kitchen and laundry, which the mistress insists must have either western or eastern light—if not both. Treat the problem as you will, keeping in mind the coveted exposures—the wish to use up some of my raw material in the shape of rocks, and withal, the desire not to make the affair too burdensomely expensive.

"P. S.—Mrs. Urban wishes a *boudoir*, which must have a south look-out too, and mind—no basement kitchen.

"P. S.—Again. Mrs. U. says the laundry might be in the basement, but not near the billiard-room, and the dairy must be convenient and cool, and the kitchen must not be too far from the dining-room, and no dumb-waiters; and it would be very nice to have a veranda for flowers, by the dining-room, and not to forget the sunny bed-room.

"She wishes a large hall, and well lighted, and servants' stairs apart, and hopes you'll place the front door in a protected situation; (south side, if possible.) And a good large China closet and butler's room, very well lighted; and bath-room convenient, on the first floor."

Fortunately a considerable slope of the land to the west admitted of the establishment of laundry and of larder (adjoining) in the basement of the kitchen extension, and also of a roomy billiard-room with south frontage, and opening westward upon the desired conservatory.

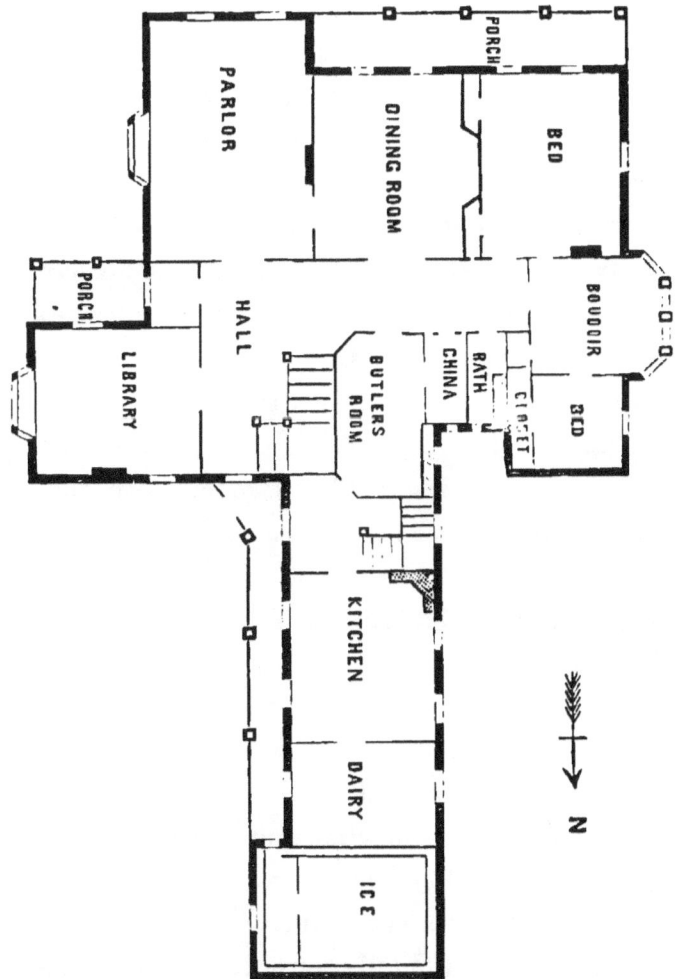

Of the floor immediately above, and upon the ground level as one approaches the place from the east, I give a rough draft, showing the general disposition of the rooms.

By this it will be seen that every considerable apartment, including even the boudoir, has a southern exposure. I give no drawing of any ground-plan, save that of the first floor, and supplement it only by a rude perspective sketch of the building, in which I have endeavored to incorporate some of the hints already given with respect to the use of homely materials and the intermingling of a timber framework with country masonry. One great advantage of this humble style lies in the fact, that it permits of the attachment of many of the rural offices (as, for instance, the ice-house and work-room above, and contiguous dairy) to the main building, without offensive contrast,—at the same time contributing to the general effect of the mass of building. Mass counts for a great deal in a country house and in landscape ; —most of all irregular mass—which can be compassed (economy considered) only by associating some of the exterior offices of a rural home with the home itself. All this, the rough material, and the simple method of combining timber framework with a rude filling-in of masonry, permits and invites.

Observe that the tall, tower-like building on the right of the view requires no expensive interior finish ; it covers offices which must be provided in some form. By attachment to the main structure it gives dignity and extent; and if it be covered with

graceful, climbing plants, it adds wonderfully to the general effect.

The outline and the tints of a country house, as I have already urged, are the great things to be reckoned, when we rate landscape effects. It is quite possible that the finesse and precision of the city architect will tell no story upon a brook side, or on such slope of land as Mr. Urban has chosen for his site. Effective building of a country house wants a picture-maker as much as architect. First, and chiefest of all, every convenience must be supplied—all sunny exposure made available—all juxta-positions reconciled—all home-like qualities guarded. Next, the mass of building must tally with the landscape, and illustrate it with a rich, good color of *home*. Outline must not be monotonous or heavy, but varied and piquant : roofs must gleam a welcome, porches promise hospitality, and chimney-tops, showing pennants of smoke, lift up standing invitations.

Conclusion.

HAVING thus presented—as it were, by turn of kaleidoscope and probably by wearisome repetition—all the shades and outlines of the fifty-acre purchase which my friend Urban has had in mind, I cannot close without a summing up.

All that I have laid down in way of design, whether for walks, plantations, or country-house, has been intended for suggestion rather than literal fulfilment. Every locality must have its own interpretation at the hands of the artist. Method must vary—not only as the hills and the slopes vary, but as the wants and the tastes of the occupant vary.

There are farms I know, unctuous with an accumulated fertility, and with right lines running athwart their slopes, which might be converted into charming park-lands, with every grass-field rounded into a lawn; but, to my eye, they would gain nothing, if in this conversion the economic interests of the holder were ignored. Land does its best service where it best feeds our human wants: not necessarily gross wants, but all wants,—fine as well as gross.

I have endeavored to demonstrate that economic management need not necessarily offend against the rulings of good taste. I feel sure that the highest beauty of landscape will ultimately bring no loss; and I forecast confidently the time—perhaps a century hence—when all the beauties and all the economies and all the humanities will be in leash.

Again, a country home will not yield its largest enjoyments to any who adopt it in virtue of a mere whim; there must be love; and with love, patience; and with patience, trust. This mistress who wears the golden daffodils in her hair, and the sweet violets at her girdle, and heaps her lap every autumn time with fruit, must be conciliated, and humored, and rewarded, and flattered, and caressed. She resents capricious and fitful attentions—like a woman; receiving them smilingly, and sulking when they are done.

I would not counsel any man to think of a home in the country, whose heart does not leap when he sees the first grass-tips lifting in the city court-yards, and the boughs of the Forsythia adrip with their golden censers. Many a man mistakes a certain pleasurable association of his boyish days with the country, for an earnest love; it may well be only a sentiment which will wilt with the scorching heats of August, and die utterly when the frosts nip the verdure of the year.

A man may take his business to the country—whether as manufacturer, stock-breeder, tobacco-grower—and decorate his business with country charms; but the retired citizen cannot go there, and find enjoyment, except he have an ineradicable love for such charms—except he can read lovingly such books as those of Walton, or White of Selborne.

I quote, in closing, a verse by that "excellent preacher and angler," Phineas Fletcher; there is a heavy British mildew on the lines; and the country-

man bepraised by the poet would not surely make a
very active railway-director; and yet the mouldy old
British portrait will not serve badly as a pendant to
these Rural Studies :—

> No empty hopes, no courtly fears him fright,
> No begging wants his middle fortune bite,
> But sweet content exiles both misery and spite.
>   His certain life, that never can deceive him,
>   Is full of thousand sweets, and rich content ;
>   The smooth-leaved beeches in the field receive him
>   With coolest shade, till noontide's heat be spent :
> His life is neither tossed in boisterous seas,
> Or the vexatious world, or lost in slothful ease :
> Pleased, and full blest he lives, when he his God can please.

THE END.

HE undersigned have associated themselves for the conduct of Landscape Gardening, and its connected branches of business — including Rural Architecture and Engineering, with the Agricultural, Horticultural, and Sanitary treatment of public and private grounds.

They will furnish designs for the laying out of Parks, Cemeteries, Farms, Country Seats, and Village Homesteads. They will also plan modifications of country houses and of old-established gardens or farms, and devise whatever, in their view, may be needful—by plantations, thinning of wood, re-adjustment of buildings or enclosures, drainage, and establishment of walks or drives —for the full development of country property, whether the proprietor aims at economic management or picturesque effects.

Simple suggestions, surveys, drawings, and specifications, for the above objects, with estimates of cost, will each or all be given, as correspondents may wish.

They further propose to give attention to the Selection of Sites, whether for Summer Houses, permanent Rural Residences, or Farms. In this connection, they propose to inaugurate a general bureau of information in regard to country homes—to advise respecting the desirableness of particular localities—whether on sanitary or economic grounds—and to negotiate transfers of country property. Correspondence is invited from those having such property for disposal ; none, however, will be offered by them, unless previously visited and examined by a member of the firm, in order that an intelligent opinion can be given of its adaptation to the special wants of a client.

MR. RICHARD M. HUNT has kindly permitted the association of his name with the firm as advising Architect.

DONALD G. MITCHELL, (of New Haven.)

WILLIAM H. GRANT,

Late Superintending Engineer of Central Park.

CITY OFFICE, STUDIO BUILDING, 51 West Tenth St., N. Y., where a member of the firm can be consulted on Saturdays, Mondays, Tuesdays, and Wednesdays ; or MR. MITCHELL may be addressed by mail at New Haven, Ct. ; MR. GRANT at Sing Sing, New York.

MY FARM OF EDGEWOOD.

By DONALD G. MITCHELL.

1 vol. 12mo., on Laid Tinted Paper. Price, $1 75.

A new issue now coming from the press for the Spring Trade.

"The cultivation of the scholarly gentleman shows itself in every page, and a sunny geniality of soul throws a softening tint over the ordinarily unpoetical and angular characteristics of agriculture."—*Evening Post.*

"The instruction which it embodies will be none the less valued because of the desultory method which the author has followed, or the many digressions into which he has been beguiled. By the great mass of readers, these very features will be considered as an additional charm. The light and easy movement of the author's style, the graceful and delicate transitions which he makes, the quiet humor in which he so naturally indulges, the sly but good-natured satire which seems to drop so naturally from his pen, and the unaffected yet chastened pathos into which he rises for a moment, are all exquisitely wrought into a varied and beautiful tissue, which is fitted to give perpetual delight to the cultivated reader, and to be itself an instrument of culture to the unrefined."—*New-Englander.*

"It is a book whose merit can hardly be over-praised. It should be in every farmer's library, as a volume full of practical advice to aid his daily work, and full of ennobling suggestions to lift his calling into a kind of epic dignity."—*Atlantic Monthly.*

"Mr. Mitchell has unusual skill in putting his experience, his culture, his taste, his delicate perceptions, into such literary forms as to make them of use to others. This work has the vitality which springs from a love of and acquaintance with nature, and will long be read as one of the best and pleasantest pictures of a New-England farm, and of the charms and drawbacks of our New-England country life."—*North American Review.*

BY THE SAME AUTHOR.

WET DAYS AT EDGEWOOD,

WITH OLD FARMERS, OLD GARDENERS, AND OLD PASTORALS.

1 vol. 12mo. Price, $1 75.

We have no more graceful writer of the English language living than the author of "My Farm" and "Wet Days at Edgewood," nor has the grace of his pen been more apparent in any of his works than in these two bucolics. In the last we have the fruits of his readings and musings among the authors who have written upon rural life and its occupations, philosophers and poets, from Hesiod and Homer down through the ages, to Charles Lamb, and Loudon, the encyclopædist. A great amount of quaint and pleasing reading is gathered from the thoughts of a hundred writers, and, by the skilful hand of our author, their seeds are cultivated into attractive plants which will beguile many an hour in town or country. The book is divided into nine "wet days," each one of which has its own attractions. The multitude of Ik Marvel's readers will join us in the wish that he may long live to write such pleasant books.

Copies sent by mail, postpaid, on receipt of price, by C. S. & Co.

DOCTOR JOHNS:

BEING A NARRATIVE OF CERTAIN EVENTS IN THE LIFE OF A CONGREGA-
TIONAL MINISTER OF CONNECTICUT. By DONALD G. MITCHELL, author
of "Reveries of a Bachelor," "My Farm of Edgewood," &c., &c.

2 vols. 12mo. Price, $3 50.

"The work affords a rare picture of New England life and manners.
It is every way a charming sketch, and must improve the mind and heart
of every one who reads it."—*Episcopalian*.

"The book shows the blended powers of the student, the thinker, the
poet, and the humorist, and is read as we read Addison or Goldsmith,
with tranquil delight."—*Boston Transcript*.

"As a piece of rhetoric, it is charming, of course; for no American
writer, since the days of Washington Irving, uses the English language as
the '*Ik Marvel*' of a few years since, and the 'Farmer of Edgewood'
of to-day."—*Round Table*.

"It is quite evident that, personally, the author has no sympathy with
the theological system which 'Dr. Johns' is made to represent, and which
is drawn in its hardest and extremest form; but still his sturdy sense of
justice makes him to describe him as a really noble character, of which
no school of orthodoxy and no church has need to be ashamed, and one
which commanded the profoundest respect and lifelong confidence of the
worldly Maverick."—*Hours at Home*.

"No book of the author seems to us so good. The great charm of it
lies in the truthfulness of its picture of New England life."—*New Haven
Palladium*.

"In one respect Dr. Johns can be spoken of with unalloyed approval;
it is a picture of life and manners that were of a social state that is fast
passing away, the mere shadows of which are on the land."—*Boston
Traveller*.

"The doctor is a kind, unworldly man, and the most interesting person
in the book; his life has been shadowed and softened by sorrow, and he
learns to love the little Adéle, though she is a Roman Catholic, and by his
love converts her to Protestantism. With his rebellious and warm-heart-
ed son he has a sadder experience: the boy, driven from home by his
father's apparent, and his hard old aunt's real, harshness, drifts about the
world, doing nothing bad, but tossed and worn by religious doubts and
love for Adéle, till at last he finds rest in perfect reconciliation with his
father, the knowledge of Adéle's love for him and death."—*Daily Spy*.

"He has evidently seen, face to face, much of what he describes. His
characters stand out clear, distinct, and life-like, with their several features of worldly wisdom, shrewd common sense, kindly feeling, exuberance of spirits, precise manners, and unfeigned piety. In dealing with
these the author is quite at home, and his delineations are at once graceful
and truthful."—*N. Y. Evangelist*.

Copies sent by mail, postpaid, on receipt of price, by C. S. & Co.

www.ingramcontent.com/pod-product-compliance
Lightning Source LLC
Chambersburg PA
CBHW020809060726
47498CB00017B/1331